FOR THE THRILL

Janis Reams Hudson

A KISMET™ Romance

METEOR PUBLISHING CORPORATION
Bensalem, Pennsylvania

KISMET™ is a trademark of Meteor Publishing Corporation

Copyright © 1992 Janis Reams Hudson
Cover Art Copyright © 1992 Jacqueline Goldstein

All rights reserved.

No part of this book may be reproduced, stored in a retrieval system, or transmitted in any form, by any means, including mechanical, electronic, photocopying, recording or otherwise, without prior written permission of the publisher, Meteor Publishing Corporation, 3369 Progress Drive, Bensalem, PA 19020.

First Printing August 1992.

ISBN: 1-56597-018-7

All the characters in this book are fictitious. Any resemblance to actual persons, living or dead, is purely coincidental.

Printed in the United States of America.

To the Cozy Café in Meeker, Oklahoma, its staff, its patrons, and its jukebox, for sparking the idea for this story . . .

And in gratitude and friendship to Cindy Hamilton of Shawnee, Oklahoma, book seller *extraordinaire*, and a willing fount of information on rodeoing. If I got things right, it's because Cindy helped me. If I made mistakes, they are my own. Thanks, Cindy, for everything.

JANIS REAMS HUDSON

Janis Reams Hudson is a two-time *Romantic Times* Reviewer's Choice Award nominee for her first book, **FOSTER LOVE** (Kismet #29). A Co-founder of the Oklahoma chapter of Romance Writers of America, Janis is active in several local writers' organizations and is currently serving a two-year term on the national Romance Writers of America Board of Directors. She lives in Oklahoma City with her husband, Ron.

Other books by Janis Reams Hudson:

No. 29 *FOSTER LOVE*
No. 72 *COMING HOME*

ONE

Maggie Randolph refilled Dutch Holstedt's coffee and stuffed her order pad back into the hip pocket of her jeans. Over the rattle and cough of the air-conditioning unit up high in the west wall, she heard the bell above the front door jingle. She sighed. Another customer, and it was only six-thirty. Where were they all coming from this morning?

With a deep breath, she summoned a smile and turned to greet the latest arrival. Eyes so dark a brown they were nearly black held her frozen to the spot. Laughing eyes that held a hint of challenge. Flirtatious eyes that said *I dare you*. Cocky eyes to match the cocky grin curling a pair of lips that did things to her breathing.

Where had all the air in the room gone? Maggie couldn't seem to draw a breath. She concentrated and finally drew air into her lungs. With the air came sanity.

Sure, okay, so he was gorgeous. If one liked the rugged, outdoor type. The cowboy look.

Only on him it wasn't just a look. Maggie could spot

a gen-u-ine, dyed-in-the-wool cowboy a mile away, and this was one, from his white hat with the beaded hatband, to his white western shirt that emphasized his dark skin, on down faded jeans to a pair of scuffed ropers.

Of course, if the clothes and the cockiness hadn't given him away, the belt buckle would have. He was the rodeo cowboy, with the prize buckle to prove it.

How did men bend over with that huge oval of silver at their waist? Turn that thing inside up, and she could serve two eggs, bacon, grits, and biscuits and gravy on it and still have room for an orange slice and a parsley sprig.

Then there was the sling holding his left arm across his chest. Of course, that could be the result of just about anything, but Maggie would bet dollars to donuts he'd banged up his arm in a rodeo.

When she caught herself listing all the various rodeo-related accidents that could have necessitated the sling, she took another deep breath. The man's injury was none of her business. Maybe it wasn't caused by rodeoing. Maybe he'd been in a car accident or pulled a muscle loading hay into a pickup. Maybe he had tripped over his own feet.

She didn't care. Why should she care?

Her gaze roamed back up to the man's face. Raven-black hair so dark it flashed blue where the light hit it fell with a slight wave to cover the back of his collar. Copper-dark skin gleamed smoothly over high cheekbones hinting at Native American blood.

And those lips. Full and sensual, they made a woman wonder . . . things Maggie had no business wondering. Especially not about a damn cowboy.

He looked vaguely familiar, but she couldn't put a

name to him. She shrugged. Probably met him at one of Steve's rodeos, or right here in the café.

His grin widened.

Good grief. Here she stood, staring at him like an idiot!

With a jerk and a slosh of coffee in the pot still in her hand, Maggie looked away and rushed toward the kitchen. What in the world had possessed her to stand there and stare at him like that?

By the time she hit the swinging doors her cheeks felt on fire. She would have pressed her hands to them, but she still held the coffeepot. With a hiss of irritation, she stepped back out of the kitchen and put the pot on the warmer. She didn't have time to hide in the kitchen; she had work to do.

"Order up, honey," Aunt Ann called from the kitchen window.

Maggie grabbed the plate, grateful for something to do to keep her from having to immediately wait on the cowboy. She swiped a pitcher of syrup off the counter and carried it and the short stack to table three. "Can I get you anything else?" she asked the truck driver.

"Some more coffee when you get a minute."

"Sure thing."

On her way to retrieve the coffeepot for the trucker and a glass of ice water for the cowboy, the front door bell jingled again. Clint Sutherland sauntered in and joined the black-headed cowboy in booth six.

At the counter, Maggie grabbed the handles of two coffee mugs with her index finger, then stood two tumblers of ice water in that hand. With the other hand she grabbed the coffeepot. After refilling the trucker's coffee, she took the water and mugs to booth six.

"Morning, Clint. How's the campaign going?"

Clint Sutherland smiled at her. "Mornin', Maggie. The campaign's getting ready to enter a new phase, now that Alex is here."

Feeling like an idiot, Maggie set the water before them and filled the coffee mugs. Alex Dillon. Clint's cousin. No wonder he had looked familiar. "How are you, Alex? I'm sorry I didn't recognize you when you first came in."

"You remember Maggie, don't you?" Clint asked his cousin.

Maggie's gaze rose slowly from the steaming mug of coffee to meet Alex's brown-black eyes. *Alex Dillon. Alex Dillon.* Something tickled the back of her mind, some thought or fact about him she should know but couldn't remember.

Up close his left cheek looked puffy, the eye above it, too. A raw scrape decorated the jaw beneath.

Alex cocked his head to one side. "Hazelwood, right? Mort's daughter?"

Maggie gave a tired smile. "Right." Why was it she was always identified as Mort's daughter, Steve's wife—sometimes people even remembered to refer to her as Steve's widow—Noah's daughter-in-law, or Stephen, Doug, or Cindy's mom? When would she ever be her own person?

Alex grinned at her. "I should have recognized that red hair of yours."

Alex Dillon. Alex Dillon. What was it she couldn't remember? She filled his coffee cup, then Clint's.

"Actually," Clint said, "as soon as Alex takes over the feed store, I can get serious about campaigning."

"Serious?" Maggie said with a smirk. "As if you haven't been running yourself ragged already, between the store, the campaign, and finishing up your term as mayor. Lacey says she hardly sees you these days."

"Well, she can see more of me now that Alex is here. Although," Clint said eyeing his cousin, "how much good he'll be with that bum shoulder, I don't know."

Alex shrugged. If Maggie hadn't been staring right at him—what *was* it that teased her mind?—she might have missed the way his mouth whitened in obvious pain at the movement.

"I told you," Alex said, "it's nothing."

"That's why your arm's in a sling," Clint said.

Injuries. Whatever it was she couldn't remember about Alex Dillon had something to do with injuries.

"Heck, no." Alex grinned at Maggie. "I wear the sling to get sympathy from the ladies. How'm I doin', darlin'?"

Maggie gave him a frown. Although she should be used to it, living in Deep Fork, Oklahoma, all her life, she hated being called cute names by people she didn't know well. "Depends on how big a truck it took to put you in that shape, *honey*. If it was just a pickup, forget it. But a semi . . . I could work up some real sympathy if you've been run over by a semi."

Alex laughed and winked. "Shucks, sugar—"

Maggie ground her teeth.

"—no puny semi could have done this much damage."

Dillon. Injuries. Steve. It had something to do with Steve.

"No, this little sling was a personal present from two thousand pounds of the rankest—"

"Bull," Maggie said. A tight, cold knot formed in the pit of her stomach. "You're a bull rider."

"Ah, hell, Alex," Clint said. "You didn't get that riding a bull. If you'd been *riding* the damn thing, instead of landing on your tail in the dirt, it wouldn't have happened."

"If I'd landed on my *tail* it wouldn't have happened," Alex said with a grin. "But I made the ride. That's what counts."

"But did you win?" Clint asked.

The cowboy Alex Dillon preened like a peacock at mating time. "Of course."

Maggie felt her hands turn to ice. "What can I get you for breakfast this morning?"

Alex gave her a puzzled look that could have had something to do with the frost in her voice. She dropped her gaze to her order pad and started scribbling. As soon as she had their orders, she fled.

Alex watched those stiff feminine shoulders disappear behind the swinging kitchen door. "Was it something I said?"

Clint swore.

"What? She stiffened up like a fence post and nearly froze me to death with one look."

"I can't believe I joked with you in front of Maggie about falling off a bull."

"What's the big deal?"

"Sometimes I forget who she was married to," Clint said darkly.

"You lost me, cuz."

"Maggie's married name is Randolph. As in Steve Randolph."

It took a minute for Alex to place the name, but when he did, he remembered everything. Steve Randolph had been one of the top bull riders in the state.

Alex hadn't been present the day Steve had flown off that bull's back and been stomped to death, but he had heard every gory detail. Stories like that were ones bull riders didn't care to hear but couldn't help listening to. Over and over. Just the way the bull had stomped Steve Randolph, over and over.

A coldness crept into his shoulder and made it ache.

Then he remembered something else from those old grisly tales. Steve's wife had been at the arena that day. "She saw it happen, didn't she?"

"Yeah," Clint said. "And she was eight months pregnant at the time."

A sick feeling grew in Alex's gut. "And she never got over it, even after . . . hell, it's been six years, Clint. She still reacts like that just to the sight of a sling after six years?"

"It's how you got the sling. Maggie hates rodeo cowboys."

"She never remarried?"

"No, but trust me. You don't care. Do yourself and her a favor and steer clear of her."

Steer clear of her. It sounded like good advice to Alex. Until he remembered the way he had felt just looking into her eyes when he'd first walked into the Corner Café less than half an hour ago. He'd felt heady, suddenly hot. Excited. He'd felt alive. Every bit as alive as he felt on the back of a bull with the roar of a Sunday crowd in his ears.

And that was something to think about. No other woman had ever affected him so strongly with her eyes, or anything else. Alex had never been the one-woman type, had never been serious about a woman. Not since eighth grade, anyway, when he'd had a crush on his American history teacher. Mrs. Clausen had had nice eyes, too. But they weren't green. When, he wondered, had he developed such a fetish for green eyes?

Maggie Hazelwood Randolph's eyes packed one hell of a punch.

When she brought their orders and refilled their coffee a few minutes later, he tried to catch those eyes, but she wouldn't look at him. Nor would she meet his gaze when he and Clint paid their ticket.

Alex was tempted to say something, just to get her to look at him, but he held his tongue. He didn't mind her not looking at him. In fact, he rather liked the view when she turned her back and walked away in those skintight jeans. The way that order pad twitched in her hip pocket with every step she took stirred his adrenaline, not to mention other things.

Steer clear of her?

Maybe. Then again, maybe not.

Outside, the September sun beat down with a vengeance, totally disregarding that it was only seven in the morning. Alex settled his hat to the best angle for shade.

"So how long are you going to be in that sling?" Clint asked as they walked the two blocks to the feed store.

"Not long," Alex said, wishing he hadn't worn the damn sling. But his doctor had sufficiently put the fear of God into him this time.

You were lucky, Dillon. You didn't separate the shoulder, just bruised it. I'm telling you, one more shoulder separation could leave you crippled for life. As it is, you're in for a lot of pain in your later years, I can guarantee it. Face it, Alex. It's time to give up bull riding. For you, past time. If that hoof had landed a few inches over, I'd be in the morgue right now looking at your crushed windpipe and broken neck.

No, the doc hadn't minced any words, which was one reason Alex was glad he had agreed to manage Sutherland Feed and Seed while Clint campaigned for state representative. Maybe it was time to see how the rest of the world lived, the world outside the rodeo.

Maybe it was time to admit thirty-eight was too old to be climbing onto the backs of rank bulls just to see if he could stay on for eight seconds. Maybe it was time for Alex to seriously think about settling down, finding a little place of his own, raising a few horses, training them. Working stock, that was the thing. Cow ponies, roping mounts, cutting horses. Yeah, maybe it was time to give up bulls.

And maybe you're just scared, Dillon. Too scared after that last fall to get back up on a bull. Scared. Lily-livered, like your old man.

"Alex?"

With a start, Alex realized he'd stopped walking and missed half of what Clint had been saying. He hurried across the street after his cousin. "Don't worry about the shoulder," Alex told him. "I'll pull my weight."

"Never thought you wouldn't."

Alex took a deep breath of hot, humid air and let a pair of green eyes into his mind. He would much rather think about Maggie Randolph than his questionable future.

He and Clint reached the edge of the feed store parking lot before Clint spoke again. "Where's that ornery stallion of yours these days?"

Alex let the mention of Cody lead him away from the green eyes and fiery hair in his mind. "He's standing stud down in Norman. When he's through, I'll have to find a place to keep him."

"Plenty of places around here. Ask around, you'll find something."

Funny, Alex thought, how attached a man could get to a horse. He missed Cody. It would be good to have him close by again. Maybe sticking in one spot for a while had more benefits than Alex had realized.

A pair of green eyes flashed in his mind.

Yeah. Benefits.

But then, who was he kidding? Maggie Randolph had home and hearth, marriage and family written all over her. And she sure wouldn't want to get tangled up with another bull rider. Not after what had happened to her husband.

Still, he knew when he slept that night, the eyes that haunted his dreams would be green.

Alex spent the morning with Clint, getting the lay of the feed store and what Alex's new position as manager would entail. It wasn't as if Alex needed the lessons. Hell, he'd practically grown up at Sutherland Feed and Seed back when Clint's dad had owned it. Alex may have grown up down the road in Meeker, but he'd spent a considerable amount of his youth in Deep Fork with Clint.

Lord, the scrapes the two of them had gotten themselves into as youngsters. They had received whippings and awards, punishment and hugs, side by side for years. But Clint had turned civilized on him a few years back and gotten himself elected mayor of Deep Fork. Now, here he was again, running for state representative this time, and with a new wife to boot.

Alex didn't like thinking about Clint and Lacey. Every time he saw the two of them together, so obviously in love with each other, Alex's own life seemed that much more bleak and empty.

But his life *wasn't* bleak and empty, damn it, and he resented feeling like it was. He had his horse, he had his plans, he had the rodeo. He had rodeo pals in damn near every state west of the Mississippi.

And you've got a bum shoulder.

Alex met the echo of doom and reason with a scowl. He didn't want to think about his shoulder, or his fear, or his future. He just wanted to light in one place for a while to see what it was like. That's why he had agreed to manage the store while Clint campaigned for office.

So if he was going to stick around, there were things he needed to do. "All right if I park my trailer out back and hook it up?" he asked Clint.

"You're going to live in that sardine can?"

Alex shrugged. His shoulder reminded him he shouldn't have. "I'm used to it."

Clint shook his head. "Be my guest. There's electrical outlets on all the utility poles around the corral. Help yourself to the juice. I doubt if you'll use enough to make a difference in the electric bill."

"Thanks." Alex nodded.

While Clint finished some paperwork so as not to leave any loose ends for Alex to deal with, Alex backed his travel trailer beneath the cottonwoods behind the corral. He had set up camp so many times over the years, always moving from one rodeo to the next, one ranch to the next between rodeos, that the process of leveling the trailer and hooking up to power took him only a few minutes.

He wandered back into the store and waited on a few customers until Clint closed up for the day. The two headed back up the sidewalk, but when Clint invited Alex to dinner at the house with Lacey, Alex declined.

"Nah, you two aren't going to have much time together when you really start campaigning next week. There's a chicken fried steak with my name on it up at the café. I'll see you in the morning."

But at the café, Alex was disappointed to discover the only two waitresses on duty had brown eyes. Maggie Randolph wasn't around.

* * *

Maggie woke abruptly with a gasp. She'd been dreaming. But what nighttime visions could have awakened her at—the bedside clock read 2:20 A.M.? She groaned in frustration and turned her back to the clock. Four-thirty came early enough without waking up two hours early.

It was only then she realized she was dripping in sweat and breathing hard. And there was this funny feeling down low in her body. Kind of hot and tingly and . . . and . . .

Oh, good grief!

Had it been so long since she had been physically turned on that it took her this long to recognize the feeling?

Yes, she thought sadly. *Yes, it has.*

Snatches of her dream danced through her mind, teasing her with half-remembered scenes—scenes that had lived only in her dreams.

She bolted upright in bed. *Good double grief!* She'd been dreaming about that damned long-haired half-breed bull rider, Alex Dillon! A man she barely knew, for heaven's sake! And not just any dream, but a *dream*, for crying out loud. Hot, breathless. Erotic.

Maggie had had cause over the past six years to hate waking up alone in the dark, but right then she was grateful for both the dark and her privacy. She could tell by the fresh surge of heat that her face was as red as a July-ripe tomato. And she knew thirty was too young for hot flashes.

Of all the unmitigated gall. How dare that itinerant cowboy invade her dreams, turn her on, then wake her up and leave her wanting?

What am I saying? She didn't want Alex Dillon! He was a stranger. If that wasn't reason enough why she had no business thinking of him, he was a good-for-nothing bull rider. It would be a cold day in hell before Maggie Hazelwood Randolph spared the time of day for a bull rider.

No sir. Not her. Not a bull rider. Not any kind of rodeo rider. As far as she was concerned, they were each and every one of them idiots. Reckless, foolish little boys who refused to grow up and become responsible adults. Risking their lives and the futures of their families for a few seconds of wild thrill they should have outgrown the need for at age twelve.

And Alex Dillon was one of them.

Steve had been, too.

Steve, whose face she saw every day in the face of her oldest son. Whose laughter she heard from the next oldest. Whose smile she saw on Noah, her father-in-law.

And though Cindy, her youngest, didn't physically resemble the father the six-year-old had never known, Maggie still suffered an ache in her chest every time she remembered the reason for Cindy's three-week premature birth.

The reason.

Come on, Magoo, you know nothing's gonna happen to me.

Steve had believed he would live forever.

It's just a rodeo, Maggie, just a bull ride. The worst I'll get is a couple of bruises if I fall off. But hell, honey, I'm not gonna fall off.

She could still see his cocky grin, his puppy-dog eyes. "Oh, Steve, why wouldn't you listen to me?"

As usual, no answer came. She was still waiting for it when the alarm went off at four-thirty. Waiting, as she had been waiting for six years, to understand why a man would take such a chance with his life. Just for fun. *For fun, damn it.*

Long before she made it to the shower she felt the need well up inside her, the need to gather her children to her and hold them close, protect them from life, keep them safe.

She called it "hovering." It happened to her every now and then, when thoughts of Steve were particularly strong, when her anger with him ran high.

She recognized the feeling but had quit fighting it years ago. Her kids hated her spells of overprotectiveness but tolerated them as "just one of those 'mother' things."

With the shower beating down on her head, the need inside her grew more demanding, the need to hover. Noah would watch her silently, knowing the cause of her actions. She knew it disturbed him that she had never forgiven Steve for getting himself stomped by that bull, but Noah Randolph believed that all things came in their own time.

He would merely watch her and give her that look of his that said, "I know what you're doing, girl, and it's crazy." He could think her crazy if he wanted, but today she was going to hover.

To give herself credit, Maggie acknowledged that her hovering spells had been coming less and less frequently. In fact, this was only the second one she remembered having in nearly a year. The only other time in recent memory had been on Cindy's birthday last month. That one was to be expected. Maggie always hovered on Cindy's birthday. It was the anniversary of Steve's death.

Maggie turned off the shower and grabbed a towel. As she blotted the water from her face she blotted out the memory of that last time she had set foot in a rodeo arena, that last ride Steve had taken, that last fall.

Thirty minutes later Maggie went to her sons' room and flipped on the light.

"Mo-om, it's too early," Stephen cried.

"Didn't I tell you?" Maggie said, forcing cheerfulness into her voice. "Aunt Ann invited you guys to the café for breakfast this morning."

From beneath his pillow, Doug mumbled.

"Get up, sleepyheads."

Doug peered out from under the pillow. "Is she gonna make us eat *grits* again?"

Maggie laughed. If only she could ensure all her children's worries were so simple. "You can eat anything you want."

Stephen sat up and rubbed the top of his head. "Anything?"

"Anything on the breakfast menu."

"Even waffles?" Doug asked. "When it's not Sunday?"

"Even waffles, when it's not Sunday."

On the way to wake Cindy, Maggie experienced a stab of guilt. She was rousing her children out of bed an hour earlier than usual, with bribes, no less, to take them to a café where they would have to stay after eating until time for school. All because Maggie felt the need to hold them close, couldn't bear to let them out of her sight one moment sooner than absolutely necessary.

By the time Maggie went downstairs, Doug was in the kitchen explaining to his grandfather about the morning's breakfast arrangements. Noah eyed Maggie over his steaming mug of coffee. "Breakfast in town, huh?"

Maggie busied herself pouring her own cup of coffee. "Seemed like a good idea."

"Did, huh?"

When Maggie turned slowly to face him, Noah's eyes were filled with quiet knowledge and sympathy. "Rough night?"

Maggie gave a jerky nod. "I guess."

After Doug ran back upstairs to hurry his brother and sister—he *would* get his waffles—Noah cleared his throat.

Maggie tensed. That was his "I've got something to say" throat clearing. And sure enough, he did.

"It's time to let go, Maggie. Past time."

Maggie tossed her hair over her shoulder. "I don't know what you mean." A barefaced lie, and they both knew it. A rough night, indeed, that had her lying to Noah.

"Yeah," he said. "Right."

Another stab of guilt hit her heart.

Damn that Alex Dillon, anyway. This was all his fault. If he hadn't invaded her dreams and made her feel things she hadn't felt in years, she could have gone on for months without one of her hovering spells. But he had made her think of sex, which made her think of Steve, the only man she'd ever—damn Alex Dillon, anyway.

An hour later, when the kids were inhaling their breakfast at booth five, Maggie damned Alex Dillon again. She had just managed to get him off her mind when she glanced out the window and saw him cross the street and head straight for the café.

Damn Alex Dillon.

TWO

Alex pushed open the door to the Corner Café and stepped inside to the tune of the jingling bell above his head and Waylon Jennings on the jukebox. The aroma of bacon and fresh coffee made his stomach growl.

He zeroed in immediately on the waitress with the red hair, green eyes, and tight jeans. She zeroed in on him, too. He would have puffed up with a swollen ego, but the look she gave him was hard enough to shatter glass.

The disgust in her eyes set his back up. Who was she to judge him? So she didn't like bull riders. His life was his own business.

So much for dreams. Those damn green eyes had teased him all night long, only to let him wake up to the reality that Maggie Randolph obviously wanted nothing to do with him.

He took the last empty booth on the east wall, right next to three kids who surely were too young to be eating in a café alone. One of them, the little girl, was so tiny she had to use a booster seat to reach the table.

The girl peered at him between the shoulders of the two boys across the table from her, whose backs were to Alex. She was a little doll, with her red hair, big green eyes, and gamine grin. Going to break some hearts when she grew up. Alex winked at her.

The little girl brought her hand to her mouth and giggled.

The two boys, arguing over who had used more syrup, ignored her.

The green-eyed waitress whacked a glass of ice water down in front of Alex. He jumped. Water splashed out of the glass and onto the table.

"Was it something I said?" he asked.

She whipped her order pad out of her hip pocket without looking at him. "Can I get you something from the menu?"

The ice in her voice did little to encourage his appetite, or anything else, for that matter, but he ordered breakfast.

"Coffee?"

He took his hat off and set it next to him on the cracked vinyl seat. "Yes, ma'am."

As she turned away from him without a glance and passed the booth next to his, one of the boys across from the little girl complained, "Mo-om, he took all the syrup."

Mom. Alex looked at the little red-haired girl with the big green eyes. He should have known. She was the spitting image of her mother.

Maggie shushed the boys and gave the little girl permission to go to the bathroom. When Maggie brought Alex's coffee a moment later—without meeting his eyes—she brought more syrup to the boys.

It was several minutes later, and Maggie was silently serving Alex his ham and eggs, when the little girl came back from the bathroom. She paused at her table, then, when her mother left, the child came and stood next to Alex.

"Hi, there," he said.

She looked at him shyly, then pointed to his sling. "You hurt your arm."

"Yeah, but it's getting well."

"Did you fall down?"

Alex grinned. "Sort of. I fell off a bull."

The big green eyes grew bigger. "At the rodeo?"

Maggie headed their way from across the room. "Cindy."

The awe in the child's voice helped make up for the ice in her mother's. "Yeah, the rodeo," Alex said. "I'm a bull rider."

"Oh." The little girl dropped her gaze to his sling again and said with the serious conviction of one who understands all life's secrets, "You're an idiot."

Alex blinked.

She looked up at him then, and Alex felt like he'd been kicked in the gut. He'd never seen a child look so . . . so solemn, so serious. In that soft little voice of hers she said, "My daddy was a idiot, too. Are you gonna die like he did?"

"Cindy!" Maggie cried with horror.

Alex felt red heat creep up his neck and face. The red heat of rage so powerful his hands shook with it.

Maggie grabbed the child and propelled her back to her booster seat. Before the woman could straighten, Alex had her by the arm and was hauling her toward the kitchen, more than aware of every eye in the place watching, every ear listening. The Corner Café was like that. Voices carried, ears perked, and everyone knew everyone else's business.

Alex stiff-armed the swinging door and marched into the kitchen, Maggie in tow.

"Alex, I'm sorry. I—"

"Lady, you ought to be horsewhipped."

"Now wait a min—"

"No, you wait. I knew your husband. Not well, but I knew him. I know what happened to him. I can understand and maybe even sympathize if you've got problems. It's a common enough thing among rodeo wives, the anger, the fear of accidents. But damnation, woman, to teach an innocent little girl words like your daughter just spouted is *wrong*. In fact, it's downright sick, if you ask me."

"Well nobody's asking you!" She jerked her arm from his grasp. "I had no idea Cindy would think such a thing, believe me."

"No idea?" Alex ground his teeth. "Where the hell did she learn it, then, if not from you? Of all the irresponsible, stupid . . . Like I said—you ought to be horsewhipped."

Chest still heaving with fury, Alex curled his lip and gave her one last glare before stomping out of the kitchen.

In a red haze of sheer rage, Maggie watched the door swing shut behind him. It was a full minute before she could speak. "How *dare* that . . . that . . . ooooo!"

She picked up the nearest empty skillet and reared back. One glance at Aunt Ann changed her mind. Aunt Ann, with that silent look that said, "Are you really sure you want to do that?"

Maggie slammed the skillet back down on the cabinet. With force.

No one had been more shocked than she when Cindy had opened her mouth to Alex. Maggie had no idea Cindy had such thoughts. She was certain she had never said anything like that within hearing of the children. She wouldn't.

Damn it, Alex Dillon had no right—*no right!*—to talk to her that way. Where did he get off telling her what she should and shouldn't teach her children?

As suddenly as her rage had come, it drained out of her, making room for something else.

"Oh, Cindy," she whispered. "Where did you get such an idea?"

Aunt Ann cleared her throat with unnecessary force.

"Well, don't look at me," Maggie cried. "I don't talk like that about Steve in front of my kids."

Ann sniffed. "Well, then. Wonder who does, if not you."

"That's what I intend to find out."

Maggie squared her shoulders and took a deep breath.

"No need to worry about the cowboy." Ann pushed a strand of gray hair back beneath her hair net. "He dropped a bill on the table and left."

Maggie felt like a bristled-up hedgehog. "I wasn't worried about him."

"Whatever." Ann turned back to the griddle. "He's gone."

Good riddance. But heavens, what had possessed Cindy to say such a thing? Maggie headed for the door to the dining room to find out, but the young lady in question poked her head into the kitchen first. "Mommy, I have to tinkle again."

This time Maggie went with her daughter into the restroom. *Lord, give me strength, give me patience, give me wisdom.* "Cindy, honey, why did you call that man an idiot?"

"The hurt man?"

How many other men have you called an idiot lately?

"Yes, the hurt man."

"Because he rides bulls in the rodeo. That means he's a idiot, doesn't it?"

"*An* idiot."

"That's what I said."

"No, I mean—" Maggie took a deep breath. "Why does that make him an idiot? Who told you that?"

Cindy cocked her head. "You did."

"*I* told you bull riders were idiots?" She hadn't. Maggie knew she hadn't. She wouldn't have said something like that to her children.

"Wellll . . ."

"Well what?"

"You told Aunt Lacey, and I heard you."

Maggie closed her eyes briefly and prayed again for strength, patience, and wisdom, but it appeared no one was listening. "I told Aunt Lacey and you heard, so you thought it was okay to say it?"

"That's right." Cindy finished her business and straightened her clothes.

"Honey." Maggie knelt to help Cindy tuck in her shirttail. "In the first place, you know you're not supposed to eavesdrop on other people's conversations. In the second—"

"What's easedrop?"

"Eavesdrop. It's when you listen to something that's none of your business. Now, as I was saying—"

"Like when I talk to my dolls and the boys listen, even when I tell 'em not to?"

"That's right. Now—"

"Spying." Cindy gave an emphatic nod. "Only with your ears 'stead of your eyes."

"Exactly. Aside from it not being a nice thing to do, it can get you in trouble."

Cindy looked up with her big green eyes. "Am I in trouble, Mommy?"

Maggie fought the urge to hug her daughter. "I'm thinking about it," she said. "But that's not the kind of trouble I meant. When you eavesdrop, you don't always hear things the way they were meant. When you heard me talking to Lacey, I was . . . I was teasing." There. That sounded good, didn't it? "Idiot is not a nice name. You know that. You don't like it when the boys call you an idiot, do you?"

"No, but it's okay, 'cuz I don't ride bulls, so I'm not really a idiot, right?"

Lord? Are you up there? "I didn't mean what I said to Lacey, honey. I was wrong to say it." *At least within your hearing.* "Your daddy was a smart man." *About most things.* "I was teasing. But when you called Mr. Dillon an idiot—"

"Is he the hurt cowboy?"

Lord? I could use a little help, here. "Yes, Mr. Dillon is the hurt cowboy, and you called him a bad name. You made him angry. You maybe even hurt his feelings."

Cindy's eyes filled up instantly. "I didn't mean to make him feel bad, Mommy."

"I know you didn't, sweetheart."

"Can I tell him I'm sorry?"

Maggie's taut shoulders relaxed a bit. No one had a bigger heart than her baby. "If you want to." She straightened Cindy's collar. "Yes. I think that would be a good idea. The very next time you see him."

"When will that be?"

"I don't know, honey." *Not too soon, I hope.*

"I didn't make him cry, did I?"

"No, I'm sure you didn't make him cry."

"Do you think he's mad at me?"

"No, he's not mad at you." *Not at you, but at me.*

"Now wash your hands and go send your brothers back here to clean up. It's almost time for school."

When Cindy left, Maggie took a deep breath. Now she was praying for calm, but it still seemed no one was listening. She had to get back to work.

But work didn't take her mind off Alex Dillon's angry words.

Imagine him accusing her of deliberately teaching her own child something like that. The jerk. She hoped Cindy *had* hurt his feelings, but she doubted he had any. They'd probably all been pounded out of him on the back of some damn bull.

Alex spent the better part of the day slinging hundred-pound feed sacks around one-handed. It didn't help. Every time he thought of that little girl's words, he saw red.

Clint came back from some errand or another around two o'clock. He walked out into the warehouse and called to Alex. "What's eating you?"

"Nothing."

"Yeah, right. That's why you're trying to throw feed sacks through the walls. You know those stacks are on pallets, don't you?"

"I know it."

"And you know we've got a forklift?"

"Is there a point to all this?"

"I'm just trying to figure out what the hell's the matter with you. Come on. What gives?"

Alex sent another bag of S & S Hen Scratch to the top of the new stack along the wall. "That woman needs her head examined."

"What woman?"

"That friend of yours up at the café. Maggie."

"What's Maggie done?"

"Of all the *stupid, irresponsible, asinine* stunts, teaching a little girl something like that." He turned to face Clint, but all he really saw was his own red haze of anger. "Do you know what that woman teaches her kids?"

"I assume you're going to tell me."

"That cute little angel of a daughter of hers firmly, seriously believes all rodeo riders are idiots—her exact word—and they're gonna die, just like her daddy did. Damn it, why would a woman teach a kid something like that?"

"Back up a minute. What are you talking about?"

Alex tossed another bag of scratch and told Clint what had happened that morning in the café.

"Ah, get off it, Alex. You don't really think Maggie taught Cindy to say that, do you?" Clint shifted his feet on the dusty wooden floor. "Hell, you know how kids are, they'll say anything."

"They repeat what they hear at home."

"Maggie wouldn't say something like that to her kids, even if she believed it."

"If? That woman's got problems, I tell you."

"Maybe she does, and maybe she doesn't. But those kids of hers are the most well mannered, polite kids in town. Ask anybody. Maggie wouldn't teach them to go around saying something like that. Besides, I don't know what you're getting so worked up about."

"I just hate to see parents teach their kids stupid fears and prejudices like that. 'My daddy was a idiot, too. Are you gonna die like he did?' Damn, I still can't believe it."

Clint gave him a narrow-eyed look. "Hit a little close to home, did she?"

Alex used his sleeve to wipe the sweat from his eyes.

And maybe to avoid his cousin's sharp gaze. "What's that supposed to mean?"

Clint shrugged. He sat on a bale of alfalfa, hands clasped behind his head, elbows sticking out, and leaned back against the bales piled behind him. "Just an idle thought, that's all. Seems like every year you're breaking a bone here, a bone there. Had that shoulder separated how many times? Maybe little Cindy Randolph got you thinking about your own mortality, and maybe you don't much like the idea."

Alex ground his teeth. "That's crap, and you know it."

Clint shrugged. "If you say so."

"Hell, Clint, I'm not afraid of getting killed in a rodeo. I never even think about it. I don't see myself getting trampled into the ground like Randolph. I don't think about it. I don't worry about it."

And it was true. He didn't think about dying.

Clint rose from the bale and headed for the door leading to the store portion of the building. "If you say so. But maybe you ought to give some thought as to just why you're so worked up over something a six-year-old said."

When the door swung shut behind Clint, Alex whirled and kicked the alfalfa bale. He had meant it when he said he wasn't worried about getting killed in a rodeo. But there were worse things than getting killed. There was fear.

Alex dropped onto the bale Clint had vacated. His shoulder ached. Hell, both shoulders ached after his fling with the feed sacks. He was hot and sweaty. And he was wondering if he even had the nerve to climb up onto the back of a bull again.

There. He'd admitted it. That's what Maggie Randolph's kid had made him face. His own fear. And he hated it. The fear of being afraid.

He didn't know if bull riding had lost some of its thrill—he'd been wondering that for months—or if he was using that idea as an excuse to quit. Because he was afraid of ending up crippled, as the doctors had been warning him for the past two years?

He shook his head. That didn't make sense. Every rodeo rider accepted the risk of injury, even death, when he made his life in the rodeo. Alex honestly did not believe he was afraid of being crippled. What he was afraid of, he thought with sudden clarity, was being afraid to ride.

Still didn't make sense.

A car pulled up out front. Another customer. He couldn't see who it was, but it didn't matter. Jeff or Tom would wait on whoever it was.

Alex leaned against the bale behind him and ignored the stiff alfalfa stalks poking through his shirt. If he wasn't afraid of dying, wasn't afraid of ending up disabled, then what the hell was there to be afraid of?

He shook his head again. "Stupid, Dillon. You're just plain stupid." There was nothing to fear. Nothing . . . except fear itself.

Alex pushed up from the bale and headed for the drinking fountain. Hell, now he was spouting quotes like some old bench warmer in front of an old-time general store. Next thing he knew, he'd be taking up whittling.

"Dillon," he told himself, "you're a jerk."

He was big and tough and mean. Everybody said so. He was a professional bull rider and a damn good one. Just because he was thirty-eight and bull riding was a young man's sport, just because the doctors had warned him to give it up, just because he had taken this job from Clint, a job that would effectively keep him off the circuit for maybe two years, did not mean he was afraid to ride again.

Of course he wasn't afraid. He wasn't a coward like his old man, a washed-up, drunken has-been. And he wasn't afraid of becoming one. He knew himself better than that.

Relieved to have that little problem worked out in his mind, he leaned down to get a drink. The door behind him creaked open.

"Alex?" It was Jeff Bonner.

"What is it?"

"Somebody here to see you."

Puzzled—not that many people knew he was in Deep Fork—Alex followed Jeff into the store. And ran smack into serious green eyes. Two pairs of them. One pair, the pair that hit him about chin level, resembled ice chips. The other, about knee-high, looked worried.

Alex nudged the brim of his hat back with a forefinger. "Ladies."

The little girl let go of her mother's hand and came to stand before him. "Mr. Dillon?"

Alex had never seen a child so serious. He squatted, more than a little leery, and met her eye to eye. What would she come up with this time? "What can I do for you?"

"I came to 'polgize. I didn't mean to call you a bad name. Are you mad at me?"

Ah, hell. How could one little kid with big green eyes and fiery red hair get to him so fast? "Naw, I'm not mad at you."

Her shy grin of relief melted something inside him.

"What's your name?" he asked.

"Cynthia. But only when I'm in trouble. You can call me Cindy if you want."

She smelled like sunshine and chalk and looked like an angel. "I'll call you Cindy if you'll call me Alex."

"Deal." She grinned and stuck out her hand for a shake.

Alex grinned back and swallowed her tiny hand with his large calloused one.

Cindy gave him a solid, no-nonsense shake, then whirled toward her mother. "Okay, Mommy, we can go get the boys now."

As the two females headed for the door, Alex rose from his squat. He waited until Cindy was outside, then called, "Mrs. Randolph?"

She halted; her shoulders stiffened. After a moment she looked at him over her shoulder. Her eyes still resembled ice chips.

Alex cleared his throat. "I was, uh, out of line this morning."

"Yes," she said, "you were."

"I'm sorry."

She raked him up and down with that hard green stare. "Yes," she said, "you are."

He hadn't expected that. He bit the inside of his jaw to keep from antagonizing her further. It didn't work. "Well, it obviously wasn't you who taught your daughter good manners."

He saw the surprise in her eyes, but that didn't keep him from turning his back and walking out on her.

He'd never met a woman with a bigger chip on her shoulder. A chip that needed to be knocked off.

Maggie lowered herself to the couch with a sigh and took a long cool swallow of iced tea as the kids streaked out the back door to go play.

"Tough day?" Noah asked from his recliner next to the couch.

"Does it show?"

"If you frown any harder your eyebrows are gonna grow together in the middle. Talk to me, girl."

She didn't want to talk to him about her day. "It's nothing. I'm just tired."

"You've been thinking about Steve again, haven't you?"

Maggie looked away from his penetrating gaze.

"It's been a long time, Maggie," he said softly. "I thought you'd gotten past all that anger."

Maggie sighed again. There was no hiding from Noah. "I thought I had, too."

"So what happened?"

Maggie shook her head. "Nothing, really. A . . . man . . . came into the café yesterday all bunged up from the rodeo, and it just all came tumbling back in on me."

Noah raised a brow. "A man?"

"Alex Dillon."

"Dillon." Noah tugged on his bottom lip. "Yeah. Bull rider from Meeker. Damn good bull rider, too. Made the National Finals the last two, maybe three years. Hear tell he does damn good on the cutting horse circuit, too."

Maggie hadn't known Alex did anything other than ride bulls, but it didn't matter. He was still a bull rider.

"He's Clint Sutherland's cousin," she told Noah. "He'll be managing the feed store while Clint campaigns, and from what I hear, he'll stay on if Clint gets elected."

Noah tugged on his lip again. "Wonder why he'd agree to do that. Ain't gonna get in much bull riding around here. Bunged up, you say?"

Maggie pictured the puffy eye, the swollen cheek . . . the lips. There was nothing wrong with Alex Dillon's lips, that was for sure. They were—*damn*. "Had his arm in a sling, a few scrapes, minor stuff."

Noah folded his gnarled hands carefully in his lap and looked at her. "So this Alex Dillon comes along, and all of a sudden you're ticked off at Steve again for dying."

A heated flush stole up Maggie's cheeks. She looked away from his pointed stare. "Stupid, isn't it?"

She felt him watching her. "Maybe, maybe not," he said. "But don't you think it's time you let go of the anger, let go of Steve? He was my son, and I miss him, too, but Maggie, there's other men out there in the world. It's time you went out and found one."

"I'm not interested in finding a man." She took another drink of tea. "You know that."

"Yeah, yeah." He waved a hand. "So you keep tellin' me. So is this Dillon character what's got you so worn out today?"

The heat came back to her cheeks. He couldn't know how she had awakened hot and aroused in the middle of the night, couldn't know she had had such a dream about a man she'd only just met. But Noah's eyes drilled into her, reading her secrets, just like they'd always done.

She took another sip of tea, then shrugged. "He's only responsible by default. What happened today was my doing."

"So what happened?"

She told him about Cindy's repeating words Maggie should never have said in the first place, and of Alex's reaction, then her talk with Cindy. She told him how Cindy had badgered her to take her to find Alex so she could apologize.

"That little sugarplum's got guts, all right. So how'd she do?"

"She did fine."

"So what's the problem?"

"The problem is me. Oh, Noah, I'm so ashamed," she whispered. "He apologized for talking to me the way he did, said he was out of line, and I . . . I threw it back in his face. I don't ever remember being that rude to anybody."

"So now you owe *him* an apology."

Maggie rolled her gaze to the ceiling, thinking idly that it was about time to paint it again. "Do I ever."

"Maybe I oughta go into town and have a look at this fellow, see what's got you so tied up in knots."

She jerked her gaze back to Noah, appalled. "Don't be silly." Why the thought of Alex Dillon and Noah Randolph together should disturb her, she had no idea, but it did. "My day had nothing to do with Alex Dillon, really. It's me. I'm the problem."

Me, and the way my heart pounds just looking at that damn cowboy.

Noah's sharp blue gaze pierced her again. "Yeah. So you say." Then he grinned.

What the devil he had to grin about, she couldn't imagine, but she'd feel a whole lot better if Noah stayed the heck away from Alex Dillon.

THREE

Alex rolled over with a groan and reached to shut off the alarm. God, he hated alarms. He'd never had much use for them until he'd come to Deep Fork and taken this job. Who ever heard of opening a store at seven in the morning?

Come on, ol' boy, Clint's gone and he's counting on you.

Get up. He had to get up. Had to help the ranchers feed their cattle, help the farmers kill their weeds.

Another groan got him sitting up on the side of the bed. Damn, six o'clock was early. The sky was barely light. He shouldn't have sat up until two playing cards with Bud Hoskins from down the street. But then, Bud was such a bad poker player, and such a happy loser, Alex hadn't been able to resist.

He stumbled from the bed to the tiny bathroom, then squeezed himself into the tinier shower, where he proceeded, with every move he made, to bash both elbows and his head against the walls. Repeatedly.

By the time he dried off—in the bedroom, because

there wasn't room to maneuver a towel in the bathroom—he felt almost human. He slipped on a pair of jeans and stood in the kitchen of his trailer. His stomach rumbled. He frowned. Damn, but he was getting sick and tired of cold cereal for breakfast.

He was, of course, perfectly capable of cooking something, but even in mid-September at this early hour, it was too warm to heat up the kitchen. And it was too quiet, the morning birds outside too sweet, for him to want to close up the windows and crank on the air conditioner.

To hell with it. He stomped back to the bedroom and dug in the bottom of his closet for a clean pair of socks. He was tired of letting an icy pair of green eyes keep him from a good hot breakfast at the only café in town.

Too bad those eyes weren't icy in his dreams. Maybe then he wouldn't care how cold and hard they got when he faced them.

But no, in his dreams those green eyes burned. For him. The lips below them softened and parted. For him. The heart beneath firm breasts pressed against his chest and pounded. For him.

With a vicious yank, Alex tugged on a boot. What the hell was he doing, dreaming about that woman? He had already established she wasn't his type. Not with hearth and home, marriage and family—complete with three kids—stamped all over her. Not with her dislike—now there was a mild word—of bull riders.

No, he didn't much care for Maggie Randolph. He'd never had much patience with or use for rude, opinionated people, and she was both. So what did he care what she thought of him?

He didn't.

He jerked on his other boot and reached for a T-shirt. He sniffed first to make sure it was clean. Sometimes he got his piles mixed up. While he snapped the cuffs of his blue shirt around his wrists, he stared at the sling hanging from the closet doorknob.

To hell with it. He didn't need the damn thing anymore. The shoulder barely hurt at all these days.

With the sky turning orange at the east edge of town, Alex walked two blocks up the slight hill to the Corner Café. The place was about half full, and he saw at once which side Maggie was working, because she turned from the table she was serving and looked at him when he entered. He took a seat on the other side of the room.

The other waitress, Barbara someone had called her, served him his breakfast. He tried not to watch Maggie. He really tried. But his gaze kept straying, pulling to her side of the room against his will. Maybe it was her tight blue jeans, hugging a pair of hips that looked made for his hands to fit around. The order pad in her hip pocket taunted him as it twitched with every step she took.

Maybe it was the way the short-sleeved sweater clung to and emphasized her breasts. Or that wild tumble of flaming hair forced back behind her neck with some sort of barrette, looking ready to explode any minute. A sharp vision of those curls cascading across his pillow started a throbbing behind the fly of his jeans.

He shifted on the red vinyl seat but couldn't take his eyes off her. Surely her carefree chatter and occasional laughter didn't draw him. He'd heard women talk and laugh before.

Then she turned and headed his way. He stared straight ahead sipping his coffee, deliberately not looking at her. He couldn't afford to look at her, to have her see into his mind and know how badly, how *fiercely* he wanted her.

"Good morning."

Her voice was soft and low. He couldn't help it. He looked at her. Her eyes were downcast. Somehow, the humble, contrite look he felt she owed him didn't seem right on her. He'd rather see her spitting fire at him. He acknowledged her greeting with a nod she probably couldn't see, staring at the table the way she was.

"I, uh, have something for you. A couple of things, actually." She dug into her hip pocket and pulled out a folded envelope. "This is your change from the other morning." She placed the envelope next to his coffee cup.

He bit the inside of his jaw. "That wasn't necessary. If I'd wanted change, I'd have waited for it."

"Well," she waved a hand. "Anyway, there it is. I meant to give it to you that afternoon at the feed store, but . . ."

He bit the other side of his jaw. *Yeah. But. You were too busy throwing my apology back in my face, weren't you, lady?*

"Uh, about . . . about what happened. I'm sorry. I was still angry about what you'd said that morning. When you apologized, I should have accepted it gracefully. Instead, I, well, I was incredibly rude." Her gaze finally rose from studying her clasped hands and met his. "So now it's my turn to apologize."

He couldn't look away from that direct stare. The urge was there to give her a little of her own medicine, to throw her apology back in her face. He had other urges, too, concerning Maggie Randolph, but they were hardly appropriate for the time and place, and they had nothing to do with apologies, those given or those thrown back. He figured after the way he'd yelled at her that morning last week, surely the two of them could call it even. There were other things he wanted to do with her besides argue. Those other things made his voice sound huskier than usual when he told her, "Apology accepted."

She gave him a slight smile. "Thank you." She stood there a moment, then asked, "How was your breakfast?"

"It was good. Does Mort still do the cooking around here?"

"Not for breakfast and lunch. Aunt Ann's back there now. Dad comes in around two. You know him?"

"Met him a time or two is all. Nice man."

"Yes, he is."

Why all the small talk? What does she want?

"I, uh . . ." She gestured with her hand toward his shoulder. "I noticed the sling is gone."

"Yeah."

She nodded. "Cindy will be glad to hear it."

"That's some kid you've got."

"Yes, isn't she?" Maggie stuffed her hands into her front pockets and rolled up onto her toes. "Well, guess I'd better get back to work. I'll, uh, see you around."

As she walked away, Alex shook his head. Who the devil understood women, anyway? Contrite and humble as she may have appeared, he'd bet his favorite hat what she really meant was, "I'll see you around, unless I can help it, cowboy."

But even that didn't stop the wanting in his gut.

Sunday morning Alex drove to his mother's in Meeker and picked up his horse trailer. His mother had gone to church, so he left her a note.

It was time to go get Cody.

He drove to the McGee-Winder Quarterhorse Ranch west of Norman where the stallion had been earning his keep at stud. His keep and, with care, part of Alex's future.

Mel Winder himself was in the stables. He ran the training end of the McGee-Winder operation, while Bud McGee handled the breeding program.

Alex and Winder greeted each other with a handshake.

"Bud's damn near frothing at the mouth, he's so excited about the foals he'll get by Cody," Winder said.

Alex grinned. "Maybe I'll up Cody's fee, then."

"Don't know why you don't start up your own operation, Dillon. You've got the firmest foundation around, with that stallion. Ought to be raising and training your own stock instead of wasting your time on those damned bulls."

Alex shrugged. It wasn't that he hadn't thought of the idea himself, but it was always "down the road." Was the idea suddenly looking more appealing, or was he looking for an excuse to give up bull riding?

No matter how many times he asked himself that question, he had no answer.

"Speaking of training," Winder said, "Russ Miller bought himself a new mare a few weeks ago. You know Miller?"

"From Anadarko?"

"That's the one. Mare seemed fine till he got her home and started workin' with her. That's when he found out she won't work for anybody but her former owner. Now he's lookin' for someone to take some of the stubborn out of her. We've kinda got our hands full around here right now. Wondered if you'd be interested in takin' her on."

Alex was a little stunned. For Mel Winder to recommend him for a job training one of his own client's horses was the highest form of praise Alex and his own skill with horses could possibly hope for. Tall and lean and wiry, Winder was a legend in the quarterhorse industry. His word and his recommendations were worth their weight in gold. Excitement shot through Alex.

Then reality sank in. He shook his head. "I appreciate the chance, but I've just taken on a full-time job managing a feed store for my cousin over in Lincoln County. That doesn't leave me much time for anything else. I wouldn't be able to spend more than a couple of hours a day training, and none at all when the days get shorter. Aside from that, I don't even have a place to keep Cody yet, except at the feed store." He shook his head again, wishing. . . .

"Well," Winder said, "you think about it anyway. Miller's not in any real hurry, and after what he heard you did with Cody, takin' him from a scrubby colt to top cutting horse, he'd pay top dollar, and you could take your time. For you, he'll wait."

Alex thanked the man, then collected his money and his horse and headed home, trying desperately not to think about starting up his own training facility.

When he got Cody back to Lincoln County, he would have liked to have taken the stallion to Clint's parents' place. But Fred and Joyce were spending a great deal of their time these days helping Clint on his campaign. They didn't need the added burden of worrying about caring for Alex's prized stallion.

Not that they would have to care for him. Alex planned to do that himself, taking care of Cody's grooming and feeding and exercising him before and after work each day. But Alex knew his aunt and uncle well enough to know they would feel obliged to check on Cody throughout the day.

He could hear Aunt Joyce now. "Fred, go on down and show that stallion where the best grass is. . . . Do you suppose you ought to show him where the pond is again? . . . The hay? . . . The oats?''

No, they didn't need to be worrying about Cody.

So Alex took the stallion back with him to the feed store. He hoped to find someplace close to town where he could board the animal, someplace he could get to easily and quickly in the mornings and evenings to groom and feed his pride and joy.

He had posted a notice on the bulletin board at the feed store last week, but so far no one had come forward with a place for him to stable and pasture Cody. For now, the stallion would have to stay in the barn and corral behind the store, but Alex hated the thought. He'd cleaned and made repairs for days, but the old facilities were nowhere good enough for a prize like Cody.

It was mid-afternoon when he unloaded Cody behind the feed store. He stroked the gleaming chestnut neck. "There you go, buddy, that ride wasn't so bad, was it?"

The horse lowered his head, looked Alex right in the eye, and snorted.

Alex rubbed the animal's ear and laughed. "Okay, so you don't like riding in a trailer. Can't say I blame you any. It's just not dignified, is it? So how were the ladies over at the McGee-Winder place, huh?"

The horse raised his nose to the sky, bared his teeth, and whinnied.

Alex chuckled. "That good, huh?" He gave Cody a pat on the shoulder, then led him into the barn. "Met one myself while you were gone. You'd like her, boy, but I don't think you'll get the chance to meet her. This lady doesn't much like cowboys, and that probably goes for their horses, too. It's a shame, 'cause Cody, I'll tell you, she's got the prettiest green eyes. You just wouldn't believe what those green eyes can do to a man."

Alex gave the gleaming coat another stroke and pat. "But I'm glad you had a good time with the women, because you're not going to like it here much. No open spaces, no running loose, no cattle to cut out of a herd. 'Course, you didn't get to do much of that for the past few weeks anyway, but you had other things to make up for it. But this won't be for long."

He led Cody beyond the small feedlot to the second corral, empty and as clean as possible now that the calves that had been there last month were sold.

"I promise," he said as he unhooked the lead from Cody's halter, "this won't be for long, boy. I'll find you someplace with plenty of grass and water, maybe some trees, and lots of room between fences. Maybe even a few cows. Would you like that?"

The horse rubbed his forehead up and down on Alex's chest.

"I thought so."

Cody nudged Alex's hand, then nipped at his shirt pocket.

Alex laughed. "All right, I guess you've earned it. You were a perfect gentleman all the way home." With two fingers Alex dug a sugar cube from his pocket.

Wednesday Clint rolled back through town and, over lunch, wanted to hear how Alex and the store were doing. Alex entered the café ahead of Clint and stood in the doorway until he figured out which side of the room Maggie was working. Call him gun-shy, but he still purposely chose the other side of the room for his eating. It seemed to make the food taste a little better when he didn't have to worry about looking directly into those green eyes. Less chance for him to make a fool of himself, too, if he didn't get close enough to touch her.

God, how he wanted to touch her. Was her skin as soft and dewy as it looked? Would her hair cling to his hand, wrap itself around his arm? Would her lips . . . *Damn*.

He spotted her on the near side, so he headed to the far. Halfway to the booth he had chosen, Clint stopped. "Hey, Noah, how's it going?"

The man was brown and leathery with gnarled hands and a friendly smile. He looked sixty but was probably much younger. Sharp blue eyes squinted and sparkled with open friendliness. "Can't complain. How's the campaign trail?"

"Long," Clint said. "Want you to meet my cousin Alex. He's managing the feed store while I'm out gallivanting. Alex, meet Noah Randolph."

Randolph. There was that name again.

The man rose and Alex shook his hand. "Good to meet you."

"Same here. Dillon, isn't it, from Meeker?"

"That's right."

"Saw you the last couple of years in the National Finals. That's some mighty fine bull ridin' you do, boy. Mighty fine. Some of the best I've seen, and I've seen my share."

Alex nodded. "Thanks. Way I hear it, you were no slouch yourself on the broncs."

Noah Randolph's chuckle gave off a dry wheeze. "That was a lifetime ago."

Alex and Clint took their seats and ordered lunch from Barbara. Every time Alex caught himself watching Maggie, he jerked his gaze back to Clint. Once, he caught Noah Randolph watching him watch Maggie.

". . . and don't forget to keep track of—"

Alex wasn't listening to Clint. He interrupted. "Any relation?"

Clint frowned. "Is who any relation to whom?"

Alex tore his gaze from that fiery head of hair across the room—well, okay, so he had been ogling her backside rather than looking at her hair—and ran into ripe speculation in Noah Randolph's eyes. Alex let his gaze slide away, sort of nonchalant-like, he hoped, until he met Clint's eyes. He met even more speculation there. "Randolph and the waitress."

Clint gave him a blank look for a moment, then the light dawned. "Noah and Maggie? He's her father-in-law. Steve's dad."

Of course. Alex should have remembered.

"Did that Purina shipment come in on time?"

Work. He had to keep his mind on work. "No. It was two days late."

"They've been doing that a lot lately," Clint said. "Their salesman's due to visit you next month. Might want to shake him up a bit. See if it does any good."

Alex nodded as he watched Maggie carry a tub of dirty dishes back to the kitchen. She perched the plastic tub on her hip. It pulled her shirt tight on one side, emphasizing the shape and fullness of one breast. Alex felt his pulse leap.

The Purina salesman wasn't the only one he'd like to shake up. Maybe he'd start sitting on her side of the room again. Just to see what happened.

When he and Clint left, Alex felt Noah Randolph's eyes all over his back. He glanced over his shoulder. The older man stared at him a minute through squinty eyes, then, with a slow, thoughtful smile and a curious twinkle in his eyes, Randolph gave Alex a nod and a two-fingered wave.

* * *

Three days later Noah Randolph walked into the feed store. He was shorter than Alex had imagined, though not short. Probably five-nine, five-ten. But the man walked just as Alex would have predicted, if he'd thought to predict. Noah Randolph walked as though he still had a horse between his legs, somewhere between a spring and a shuffle, with a little saunter thrown in, with his knees bowed out, heels in.

"Mornin'," Alex offered.

Randolph pushed his bill cap back on his head. "Hear you might be looking for a place to keep a stallion."

"Yes, sir, I sure am."

"We've got plenty of pasture and empty stalls in the barn. You're welcome to come out and have a look."

"Appreciate that. I need to tell you, though, while Cody loves people and nearly all animals, he's not too fond of other stallions."

"No problem. All I've got is a dozen head of cattle."

Alex frowned. "I thought I remembered you raised quarter horses."

"Used to." Randolph shuffled his feet and glanced at the shelves of herbicides beside him. "Sort of lost interest a few years ago. Sold all my stock."

Alex was stunned. From what he remembered, Noah Randolph had been one of the top working-horse trainers around.

"Anyway," Randolph said, "there's plenty of room for your stallion, if you're interested."

Alex didn't have to think about it. "I'm interested."

The sun blinded Maggie for an instant as she turned west along the north bank of the Deep Fork River on the dirt and gravel section line road that led to her house. It was seven o'clock and she was bone tired. Harriet had had a doctor's appointment over in Oklahoma City late in the afternoon and hadn't been able to get to work on time, so Maggie had covered for her.

It had been awhile since Maggie had put that many hours in at the café in one day. The only saving grace was that Noah had by now taken care of the kids' dinner. All she would have to contend with would be a few loads of laundry, some ironing, making sure the kids did their homework, and whatever else came up during the course of the evening. Her shoulders sagged.

Glancing toward the rise ahead on the right, to her home, she rolled down her window and took a deep breath of warm damp air straight off the river to her left. The air, the sight of the old white Victorian farmhouse standing watch over the river, the oaks and willows and pecan trees dotting the front yard with shade, all of it renewed her spirit, recharged her energy, as it did every time she came home.

Lord, how she loved the place Steve had brought her to when they'd first married. She had lived there so long, twelve years now, it seemed like she had never lived anywhere else. This, to Maggie, was home. The two-story white house with the huge red barn out back, the chicken coop, the—*the big black pickup with a matching goosenecked horse trailer?*

That's what it was, all right, parked right in front of the barn. Spotless, gleaming, black, with enough chrome to put braces on the teeth of all the children in the free world. *And someone's unloading a horse from the trailer.*

Who would have the *nerve* to bring a horse to their place? If some slick-talking stranger was trying to sell Noah a horse . . . well, it just wouldn't do. Noah knew how Maggie felt about horses. Surely he wouldn't weaken and buy one.

A twinge of guilt pierced her conscience. Noah was a born horseman. But he had sold all the stock after Steve's death—the broncs used for bareback riding, the roping horses Noah and Steve had raised and trained, the bulls Steve had practiced on. Noah had understood how she felt about anything resembling the rodeo and had readily agreed to get rid of the animals.

Maggie floored the gas pedal. No fast-talking cowboy down on his luck and looking for a quick dollar was going to talk Noah into buying a horse. Not while she had breath in her body. She absolutely refused to have her children around dangerous animals. Noah knew that. But she would put in her two-cents' worth just the same.

She slowed for the turn, then barreled up the driveway and whipped the Dodge Caravan into her parking spot behind the house, managing to keep the rear end of the van from fishtailing more than a couple of feet—she had taken the turn just a bit too fast. But damn it, she wanted to know who had the nerve to bring a horse to her house.

What she found when she got out of the van and rounded the shiny black pickup was enough to make her blood boil. Alex Dillon was leading a big chestnut stallion right up to her children! And Noah wasn't doing a thing about it! Noah knew the kids were afraid of horses. Why wasn't he stopping this?

Maggie sprinted toward her children.

What happened next happened so quickly she could do nothing to prevent it.

With Alex murmuring into his ear, the big horse stopped directly in front of Cindy, who stood sandwiched between Stephen and Doug. Her poor baby! She was probably terrified!

The horse lowered his massive head right down to Cindy's chest and snorted. Cindy let out a squeak. It wasn't a giggle; it just sounded like one from the distance. Maggie knew it couldn't be a giggle. Just like her brothers, Cindy was too afraid of horses to be giggling.

The huge beast loomed over Cindy. He stuck his face in hers, curled his lips, and bared his teeth. Cindy squealed and jumped back, jostling her brothers.

The horse jerked his head up sharply.

The abrupt movement startled Doug and Stephen. They stumbled backward.

"Get that animal away from my children!" Maggie screamed.

Three young heads snapped around toward her. Alex cocked one hip and rested a gloved hand on the neck of the gleaming chestnut stallion, who snorted at Maggie's approach. Noah . . . Noah looked like he'd just been caught with his hand in the proverbial cookie jar.

"Welp," Stephen said. "Time to go."

"You kids get in the house," she told them. She didn't have to tell them twice. They were halfway there before she finished speaking.

With trembling knees and hands like ice, Maggie faced Noah. "What is the meaning of this?"

He stretched up to his full height and threw his shoulders back. Macho. Maggie ground her teeth. Noah hadn't pulled his macho act around her in years.

"Dillon, here, is going to be boarding his horse with us."

What?! "You're not serious. Tell me you're not serious, Noah."

Noah worked his toothpick from one side of his

mouth to the other without benefit of hands. "I'm serious, Maggie girl."

It was a wonder the stiff south breeze didn't just blow her down, she was so shocked. "You'd do that to me, to us, knowing how I feel? Knowing how scared the kids are of horses?"

The toothpick made another trip across Noah's mouth. "It's time, Maggie. Past time. Dillon needs a place to board his horse, and we've got the perfect setup just sittin' here goin' to waste. And those kids aren't one bit scared."

Maggie clenched her fists at her sides. "Of course they're scared. I saw what just happened. You can't do this, Noah." From the corner of her eye she saw Alex start leading the horse toward the barn. "Where do you think you're taking that animal, mister? You just load him right back up in that trailer and get him the hell out of here."

"Now, Maggie," Noah said.

"Don't you '*now Maggie*' me, Noah Randolph." Her voice, her entire body, shook with pain and rage. How dare Noah do this to her? *Why* was he doing it? "You and I both know stallions aren't to be trusted, especially around young children who have no experience with horses. You saw how scared the kids were. I want that animal out of here, and I want him out now."

She swung on Alex. "You're doing this on purpose, aren't you?" she demanded. "You're just trying to get back at me for what Cindy said to you that morning in the café."

Alex narrowed his eyes. "Mrs. Randolph, I don't have the slightest idea what you're talking about. I thought you only had a problem with bulls."

"Bulls, horses," she waved a hand in the air, "what's the difference? They're all dangerous animals.

I won't have my children endangered or terrified because the two of you want to play cowboy."

"Lady," Alex said softly, "you're nuts."

"You purposely let that animal terrorize my children."

"Terrorize! I did no such thing," he cried. "Noah told me they'd never been around horses. I was trying to introduce them to each other until you came up here screeching like a banshee. They'll need to get used to Cody before they can ride him."

Maggie's heart nearly stopped. "*Ride him?*" she shrieked. "My children won't be learning how to ride, Mr. Dillon. Most especially not that horse." She tossed the stallion a glare. "Because that horse, and you along with it, are leaving. Right now."

"Hold on, there," Noah said. "I invited Dillon to keep the horse here, Maggie."

"Well, you can just uninvite him." She folded her arms across her chest so the two men wouldn't see how badly her hands were shaking.

"No," Noah said, "I won't."

Maggie reeled. Noah had never denied her anything, had never tried to interfere in how she raised her children, had never gone against her wishes like this.

"Maggie girl," her father-in-law said softly. "No one loves you more than I do, you know that. And you're the only one alive who loves those kids more than I do. I know what you're doing, what you've been doing for six years. You're trying to protect the kids from getting hurt. That's what mothers are supposed to do. But Maggie, you're trying to teach them to be afraid of things all their friends take for granted. It ain't good, Maggie, it ain't right. Besides," he admitted, "it ain't working. You didn't see their faces when Alex told them they could pet Cody."

"I didn't have to see their faces. I know how scared they are of horses." She raised her eyes to the sky, hoping the wind would dry the gathering tears.

"They're not as scared as you think they are," Noah said. "The horse stays."

"Don't my feeling or the kids' count for anything anymore?"

"You know they do. Like I said, I love you and those kids. You're what I live for. If you ever decided to take them and leave, I don't know how I would go on. But Maggie," he added softly, "I've got some say around here, you know. This is my home, too."

Betrayal stabbed sharp and deep. Maggie reeled as though she'd been slapped. With a hand over her mouth, she turned and ran for the house.

FOUR

Alex's grip on the lead line tightened, and Cody picked up on the fury racing through him. The stallion danced around and tried to toss his head. Alex gave the lead a yank, all the while watching Maggie race across the yard to the back door of the house. He didn't know who he wanted to strangle first, the woman or the old man. He waited until the back door slammed shut behind her, then slowly, carefully tied Cody's lead to the corral fence.

Then he turned to the man beside him. "You used me, Randolph. I don't much like being used."

Randolph looked him straight in the eye. "You needed a place—"

"Cut the crap, old man. You knew exactly how she'd react to having a horse here. You used me to rattle her cage, and we both know it."

"Yep." Randolph gave a sharp nod and rocked back on his heels. "That I did."

"Why, damn it? Why me?"

Randolph snorted around his toothpick. "Why you?

Huh. You think I'm blind? I've got eyes in my head, boy. It appears to me you've been wantin' to do a little cage rattling of your own. I'm just giving you the chance."

Alex was at once appalled, suspicious, and stunned. "Why?"

Randolph merely shrugged.

Alex cursed. "If you had any protective instincts toward that woman at all, you'd be running me off with a shotgun."

The old man raised his face to the sky and laughed.

Maggie hid in her bedroom upstairs and peeked through the crack in the curtains. When she saw Noah laugh at something Alex said, it felt like a knife stabbing straight to her heart. She felt . . . betrayed.

She felt even more betrayed a moment later when the two men led the stallion into the barn. A blanket of ice settled over her. Then came the anger. Anger at Noah for so blatantly going against her wishes. Anger at Alex Dillon for . . . for . . . *for drawing breath*.

Of course, Noah's betrayal wasn't as bad as the one her kids had dealt her moments ago when Maggie had run to the house. She had sought them out to comfort their fears. She expected soothing them would take some doing. What she had found was three kids laughing over cartoons and wrestling on the floor in the den. As though nothing had happened.

It was his fault. That cowboy. If he hadn't come to town, none of this would be happening. Somehow he had finagled his way into Noah's good graces and coerced Noah into letting him bring that damn horse here. She was sure of it. Positive, in fact.

Her life had been sailing along rather smoothly until

that half-breed bull rider strolled into town. Now everything was wrong. Everything!

She watched the object of her fury climb into his shiny black pickup and back the horse trailer to the side of the barn, where he unhitched it. Then he drove off, leaving horse and trailer behind.

Damn him.

Maggie whirled away from the window and threw open her bedroom door. If she didn't expend some of the energy generated by her anger, she would explode. Like a whirlwind, she circled through the kids' rooms gathering arm loads of dirty clothes.

By the time she had the first load downstairs and into the washer, she could hear Noah in the den talking to the kids. When she left the laundry room, she met them all in the kitchen. "Where are you going?" she asked the kids.

"Outside to play," Stephen said. "Is that okay, Mom?"

Is that okay? Since when did they bother to ask? "What about homework?"

They all said they didn't have any.

"All right." Then she shot them each a glare. "But if any one of you steps foot near that horse, *all* of you will get a whipping."

"All of us!" Doug cried. "That's not fair."

Good grief. Had one of them been planning to—no. No. They wouldn't. But just to make sure, she said, "Fair or not, that's the rule."

"Yes, ma'am," they chorused.

Maggie felt marginally better. At least her children were showing good sense. They knew how dangerous large animals could be. She had taught them that. But she was going to murder Alex Dillon for bringing that horse here.

Maggie tossed Noah an "I told you so" look—she was right to demand that Alex take the horse away, because her children were afraid of it. She shooed the kids out to play. "Be back in the house before dark, and don't leave the yard."

Another chorus of "Yes, ma'ams" floated through the screen door.

At the edge of the porch, Stephen turned back. "You want us to do the chickens?"

For a brief moment, Maggie felt her good humor restored. She had told the kids to be in before dark. Stephen knew as well as she did that the chickens wouldn't go to roost in the henhouse until it was dark enough for the yard light to come on. If he had to wait on them, then feed and water them and lock them in for the night, he could stay outside an extra half-hour or more by dawdling long enough.

She gave him a smile. "I'll take care of the chickens tonight. But thanks for offering."

Stephen gave her a halfhearted smile, then followed Doug and Cindy into the yard.

Maggie turned and faced her father-in-law. Her good humor evaporated. Alex Dillon may not have been near enough to murder just then, but Noah Randolph sure was. "I want to talk to you."

Noah narrowed his eyes. "Kinda figured you did."

Now that she had her chance, Maggie wasn't sure what to say. She decided to go with her anger. "I can't believe you would purposely endanger your own grandchildren this way."

"That's not fair, and you know it."

"No," she cried. "It's not fair. It's not fair that you bring that animal here knowing how I feel. It's not fair to risk my children's safety for no good reason. It's not fair for me to have to fear for their very lives right here in our own home, damn it."

"Now we're getting somewhere. Let's talk about that fear of yours. It's a little unreasonable, you know, even for you."

"Unreasonable!" She threw her hands in the air. "Damn it, Noah, it is not unreasonable, not after what happened to Steve."

"You know, I'm gettin' a little tired of you using Steve's accident as an excuse to hide from life, girl. He got thrown from a bull, not a horse, and you know it."

"I know it! I know it! But what about you?"

"What about me?"

Damn him, how could he stand there so calmly when her entire world was spinning out of control? "Do you think I want my kids to end up half crippled with stiff joints and arthritis like you? Don't try to convince me horses aren't responsible for the shape you're in, Noah Randolph, because we both know better."

The wiry, bandy-legged man who had treated her like the daughter he never had stiffened at her harsh words. Noah had so much pride. And she'd just dealt it a heavy blow with her anger and her quick tongue.

"Oh, Noah, I'm sorry."

He waved her apology away.

All right, if that's the way he wanted it. "I don't want that horse here, Noah."

"And I do. Face it, girl, we could use the money. I want the horse to stay. I gave my word to Dillon. So how are we going to solve this little problem?"

It was a dream. A bad dream, and nothing more. She would wake up in the morning and there would be no horse in the barn, no harsh words between her and Noah.

But the Noah standing before her now, with his head high, shoulders back, reminded her this was no dream. This nightmare was really happening. "I'm thinking of my children's safety, and you're talking about money?"

"Safety," Noah scoffed. "That horse ain't gonna hurt those kids."

Maggie folded her arms across her chest and stuck out her chin. "You can guarantee that, can you?"

"Just as sure as you can guarantee their school bus don't take a dive off that bridge yonder and end up in the river some morning," he snapped. "Guarantees. Huh."

Maggie spent half the night tortured by visions of the school bus full of children—*her* children—plunging off the old bridge at the edge of town, landing on its top in the muddy, swirling waters of the Deep Fork River. By the time her alarm went off her skin was clammy and she felt like she'd been run through her grandmother's wringer.

"Damn it, Noah," she whispered, "why did you have to mention school buses?"

All during her shower she fought the urge to take the kids to the café with her again so they wouldn't have to ride the bus.

"You're losing it, Magoo," she told herself in the mirror. Who was to say the vehicle in the river wouldn't be her own van, rather than the school bus? She couldn't protect her children from *everything*—not if she planned to let them out the door sometime during their lives.

Once again that feeling of her world spinning out of control gripped her. Sick fear for her children's safety tasted bitter on her tongue.

And Noah. She and Noah hadn't argued about *anything* in years.

Her life had been so simple until the day that damned Alex Dillon had come sauntering into town. Alex Dillon, with his coal-black hair, smoky brown eyes, and tempting lips—

Good grief! Tempting lips? Where the hell had that thought come from? His lips weren't tempting in the least. They were too full, too expressive, too hard looking. *Except when they smiled.*

Maggie threw her towel at the towel bar and missed.

She was not attracted to Alex Dillon. She didn't even like him. Despised him, in fact. Hated him. He was the reason her world was spinning out of control.

She resisted the urge to wake the kids and take them with her. She would let them have a normal morning of sleeping until six, then sitting down to breakfast prepared by their grandfather. There was no point in dragging them out of the house before sunup, the way she'd done a couple of weeks ago. Let their lives be as normal as possible.

For herself, Maggie feared nothing would ever be normal again.

On her way to work, she had to grit her teeth and force herself not to look down into the dark swirling waters as she crossed the Deep Fork bridge.

This, too, this newest fear, was Alex Dillon's fault.

When he walked into the café ten minutes after she unlocked the front door, she ground her teeth again. When he sat on her side of the room, she wanted to spit she was so mad.

She managed to refrain from spitting, but that didn't mean she had to be overly friendly either. She set a water glass in front of him none too gently and whipped out her order pad. She absolutely refused to look him in the face. She might end up spitting after all.

The overhead lights gleamed off his blue-black hair still damp from his shower. She dropped her gaze to his hands. Big, broad hands, surely calloused beyond any softness they might once have had. Competent-looking hands. She had to give him that much. Long blunt fingers; clean, trimmed nails. Strong-looking hands.

Maggie tore her gaze away and stared at her pad. "You gonna order?"

"Maggie?" he said quietly. "I'm sorry about the trouble last night out at your place. I didn't know how you felt about horses. Heck, I didn't even know you lived there until your kids came out of the house after I had Cody unloaded. Anyway," he said, "I'm sorry."

Maggie tapped her pencil against her pad. "Let's just drop it, shall we?"

"I don't want to drop it. I want to apologize."

"I don't need your apology. Do you want breakfast or not?"

"What I want," he said, his voice getting harder, more gravelly, "is for you to look me in the face."

Maggie ground her teeth. "I don't have time for this. I'll get you some coffee while you decide what to eat."

She turned to leave, but he grabbed her arm.

She looked at him then, with all the venom she could muster.

He glared right back. "I *said* I was sorry."

"Read my lips, cowboy. I—don't—care. You had no right bringing that animal to our place, terrifying my children."

"That cuts it." Still holding on to her arm, Alex slid out of the booth and loomed over her. "I think it's time for another trip to the kitchen for you and me, lady."

Maggie could feel every head in the room turn toward them. Sheer embarrassment kept her from fighting Alex every step of the way. But once past the swinging door, she whirled on him. "You let go of my arm right this minute or I'll scream the damned roof down. I *won't* be manhandled!"

Instead of releasing her, he pulled her closer. "And I won't be accused of terrifying little children. Suppose you tell me just how you can claim they were anything resembling terrified of a horse. They live on a damned ranch," he said through clenched teeth.

The man was evidently every bit as angry as she was, but Maggie didn't care. "What my kids are afraid of is none of your business."

"You and your father-in-law made it my business last night with that little scene in front of the barn."

"That wasn't any of your business either. Let go of my arm."

"No. Look, Maggie," he said in a more reasonable tone. "I know you haven't got any use for bull riders. That's fine. I can even understand if you're scared of bulls. Scared of the whole damn rodeo. That's natural. But in a town like Deep Fork, and on a ranch, for crying out loud, it's not natural for kids that age to be afraid of a horse."

Maggie's hackles rose. "Are you calling my children unnatural?"

"Hell no," he cried. "If you think those kids were scared last night, you don't know them as well as you think you do. As well as you should." His voice once again vibrated with anger. What did *he* have to be angry about? "Maybe you want them to be afraid, but I'm telling you, they're not."

"You're lying. A little fear will keep them safe."

"The kind of fear you've got will cripple them."

"There's nothing wrong with trying to keep my children from getting hurt. If I teach them caution—"

"You're not talking about caution, and we both know it. You're talking about fear. Unreasonable fear, from where I stand. If you want to walk around an emotional cripple the rest of your life, fine, but you've got no right to wish that on innocent children, even if they're your children. Even if it's your fear. Of all the irresponsible, *harmful* things to teach a child, unwarranted fear has to be somewhere near the top of the list. If you keep at it, keep telling them they're afraid, maybe someday they might be. If you don't lighten up on those kids, they're going to end up being afraid to cross the damn street."

Maggie was so livid she was nearly speechless. Nearly, but not quite. "Are you finished telling me how to raise my own children, you son of a—"

"Yeah, I'm finished. Tell Noah I'll be moving Cody out of your way as soon as I find someplace else to keep him."

He dropped her arm like it was something slimy. In the ringing silence after he left, Maggie blinked furiously. How dare he? How *dare* he!

Alex scooped his hat from where he'd left it in the booth and stomped out of the café, ignoring the watching eyes of the other customers. By the time he reached the feed store, his hands were still shaking with pure rage.

He needed to calm down. He had just enough time before opening the store to drive out and give Cody a quick grooming. Cody wouldn't appreciate a pair of shaking hands.

Alex climbed into his pickup and took the back roads too fast. At the Randolph place he parked next to his horse trailer and tried not to notice the three young faces peeking out a back window of the house.

Afraid. Sure.

A few minutes later, with Cody standing outside his stall, Alex took the brush in one hand and the currycomb in the other and went to work.

"I'll tell you, boy," Alex said, "that woman makes me so mad. . . . She's got problems, Cody. Real bad problems. I wish . . . well, guess it doesn't matter much what I wish. She sure doesn't want anything to do with me. Or you, either, for that matter."

Alex let the rhythmic motion of his brush strokes soothe him.

"Ah, but Cody, she sure is something. When she's mad she's like this shimmering ball of fire, with a few lightning bolts around the edges to keep things interesting. Those green eyes of hers can scorch a man clear down to his toes. And when she's not mad—Cody, you just wouldn't believe what one woman's smile can do to a man's heart. She's so—"

At a rustling sound behind him, Alex bit off his words and spun around.

" 'Mornin'," Noah said from the doorway.

Alex felt himself flush. How long had the man been standing there? "Good morning."

Noah came forward. "Meant to ask you yesterday, isn't this the stallion you won the Cutting Horse Futurity on a couple of years ago?"

"That's right." Alex changed brushes and went to work on Cody's tail. "By the way, I saw Maggie awhile ago at the café. I told her I'd be finding a new place to keep Cody."

Noah stuffed his hands in his pockets. "She and I

had that all settled last night. I told her the horse was staying. You don't have to take him off.''

Alex paused and straightened. He didn't want to find another place to keep Cody. This one was perfect, and it was close to the feed store—the closest place he would find. But he sensed the old man had ulterior motives for offering to board Cody. He just wished he knew what those motives were.

Or maybe he didn't. Maybe he was better off not knowing. Still . . . "I don't want to make Maggie uncomfortable."

Noah's eyes narrowed and his lips twitched. "You don't, huh?"

After a long look, Alex turned back to brushing Cody's tail. "What's that supposed to mean?"

"Not a thing, not a thing. Don't you worry about Maggie. She'll come around."

Alex paused and looked over his shoulder at Randolph. Now why, he wondered, did he get the distinct feeling the old man wasn't talking about Maggie's feelings for Cody? What was the crafty old devil up to? But Alex didn't ask. He merely watched as the old man sauntered out with that bowlegged, deliberate shuffle.

Maybe Alex wouldn't look too hard for another place to board Cody after all.

And maybe he was letting a pair of green eyes, and his own overactive glands, get to him.

"Let this be a lesson to you, Cody. Never fall for a pair of pretty green eyes, or tight jeans, either. They can make you do things you know you shouldn't."

Maggie stormed through the next days waiting for another confrontation with Alex, but nothing happened. Sometimes she passed him on her way to work in the mornings, when he was on his way to take care of his horse, but he didn't come in for breakfast at the café anymore.

She saw him in the evenings, after he'd closed the feed store, but only from a distance. He came every day and saddled up Cody and rode off over the hill.

As for the kids, Maggie reminded them each day to stay away from the horse. Noah gave his word he would see they obeyed when she wasn't around.

On the surface, things seemed smooth, and Maggie was grateful. But not one whit of this new peacefulness lessened her animosity toward Alex Dillon.

As election day drew closer, Maggie and her father geared up for the watch party to be held for Clint at the café. When the big day arrived, they draped red, white, and blue bunting around the dining room and hung banners from every light fixture. They had bags of confetti prepared—they *knew* Clint was going to win.

Extra soft drinks and coffee and ice were already stocked. Mort came in early and spent all morning with Ann preparing a huge cake for the occasion. The drugstore across the street had taken care of ordering party horns and noisemakers and streamers. Madison's TV and Appliance brought in a big-screen TV and set it on the front counter so everyone in the café could see it. No one would want to miss the minute Clint was declared the winner.

The place really took on a party atmosphere when the "Vote for Sutherland" committee showed up with two hundred helium-filled red, white, and blue balloons, which completely covered the ceiling.

Maggie, Mort, and Ann got so caught up in preparations they nearly forgot to go cast their votes. No one thought of it until the dinner crowd started coming in.

Maggie sneaked out the back door and ran down

Harding Avenue to the school, where she was to vote. Thank goodness there hadn't been a line, and thank goodness the district hadn't installed the new voting machines yet. If she'd had to deal with anything more complicated than pencil and paper, no telling how long it would have taken her. She wasn't away from the café more than five minutes. By the time she returned, Noah and the kids had arrived. Next Ann, then Mort slipped out to vote.

By six-thirty, with the polls not due to close for another half hour, the election watch party was in full swing. Two churches brought in extra folding chairs, and the café was packed like a can of sardines. Maggie could barely make her way between customers to serve food.

And the noise level! Patrons had to shout for Maggie and the other waitresses—everyone was working tonight.

Maggie hadn't had so much fun in years. It was like New Year's Eve and Fourth of July all rolled into one. At five after seven a shout went up. "Here he is! The man of the hour!"

"Hey, Clint!"

"Mr. State Representative!"

Maggie fought her way toward the door so she could lead Clint, Lacey, their parents, and . . . good grief, Alex was with them, and Maggie was going to have to be civil. This was the first time she'd been near enough to Alex to speak to him since their confrontation in the kitchen more than three weeks ago. She wiped her inexplicably damp palms on the thighs of her jeans.

"Magoo!" Lacey cried.

"This way," Maggie called back with a wave.

Lacey placed a hand on her husband's chest to get his attention. The look of tenderness he gave her nearly took Maggie's breath away. It stirred a deep longing in her breast for something similar.

Lacey motioned toward Maggie, and Clint wrapped his arm around his wife's shoulders and plowed his way through the crowd, answering greetings and shaking hands.

Lacey's parents and Clint's followed them, with Alex bringing up the rear.

When they drew near, Lacey leaned toward Maggie and shouted, "I haven't seen you in ages, Magoo."

"I know," Maggie shouted back. "Doesn't look like we'll get much of a chance to talk tonight. How have you held up under all this campaigning?"

Lacey grinned and looked lovingly toward Clint. "Just fine," she said. "We're both doing fine."

Clint led Lacey to the reserved center table and seated her. Both sets of parents filed past Maggie with shouts of hello and howdy. Then came Alex. He paused in front of Maggie and looked down at her. Her breath caught in her throat.

"Hello, Maggie."

His deep gravelly voice sent hot shivers racing down her spine. All she could do was nod in response. That intense look in his eyes robbed her of speech.

Then he was past her and taking a seat at the table.

The next couple of hours moved in a high-speed blur for Maggie. It wasn't likely to be a long evening, she knew. Much if not most of the voting in their district was still done on paper ballots, which had to be hand counted. Although most people assumed the new computerized voting machines sped things up, the people in Maggie's district knew better.

It wasn't long before their knowledge proved correct. Totals from polling places all over the state were delayed because the bugs hadn't been worked out of the new computer system yet.

By nine-thirty, Clint Sutherland was officially declared winner over his opponent for state representative. The shout that went up from the Corner Café was thunderous.

Everybody started kissing everybody as though welcoming in a new year.

From where she stood near Clint's table, Maggie glanced toward the kitchen door. Yes, her father was there. He spotted her and gave her a big grin. She answered with a thumbs-up signal. Mort tugged on the cord hanging from the ceiling. The surprise banner unfurled to deafening applause: CONGRATULATIONS, REPRESENTATIVE SUTHERLAND!

Maggie turned and gave Lacey a hug. "Congratulations, Mrs. Representative."

"What about me?" Clint cried. "I'm the one who won the election."

"Oh, well." Maggie laughed and gave Clint a hug. "Congratulations to you, too."

"Somebody was pretty sure of my election. Where'd that banner come from?"

"City employees chipped in."

"How sweet of them," Lacey said.

"Probably not," Clint answered with a chuckle. "They're just glad to get me out of the mayor's office."

Maggie laughed with Clint and Lacey, then turned—and ran smack into Alex Dillon's arms. She immediately stiffened.

Alex held on and leaned toward her ear. "Wait," he said. His breath tickled her cheek. "Do you think, for Clint's sake, you and I could call a truce for tonight?"

Maggie swallowed. Strange that in an overpacked,

overwarm room filled with hardworking people and too much cigarette smoke, not to mention the aromas from the kitchen, all she could seem to smell was the fresh scent of soap and outdoor air.

She glanced around the room, seeking an answer. All she saw were people kissing each other, laughing, toasting, patting each other on the back.

Alex shifted until he looked her in the eye. "Maggie?"

Her heart pounded. She managed a tentative smile. "Okay. A truce."

He leaned closer. "Good. Because now that we're friends, sort of, there's something I've been wanting to do since the day I met you."

Maggie swallowed again. "What?" She couldn't seem to look away from those dark eyes.

"This." And he kissed her. The first light touch of his lips on hers sent a shock wave of tingling electricity straight to the back of her skull and down to her fingers and toes. She gasped. Then his mouth took hers again. No tender, tentative kiss, this one. No, not from Alex Dillon. This kiss was hard and bold and fierce, and Maggie felt like she was drowning in it. It was a kiss of possession, of hungry, unapologetic wanting.

And as far as Maggie's traitorous senses were concerned, it was a kiss that ended much too soon. When Alex tore his lips from hers, she felt . . . abandoned.

She opened her eyes—when had she closed them?— and saw the stunned expression on his face. It plainly reflected her own feelings. How could this happen? How could she feel such . . . She didn't know what she felt. She only wished she didn't feel any of it. Not with this man. Not from his kiss.

"Why did you do that?" she asked. What she had

intended as a sharp demand came out a breathy whisper.

Alex looked her boldly in the eye. "Because we both wondered, both wanted it."

Maggie pushed away from him. He was wrong. He had to be wrong. She didn't want, hadn't wondered.

She felt her heart slow and her breathing calm. "What I want is none of your business. Nothing about me is any of your business. Stay away from me, Alex. The truce is over."

FIVE

Alex watched Maggie weave away from him, through the crowded, smoke-filled dining room. She was wrong about one thing. *Everything* about her was his business. He was going to see to it. No kiss in his life had ever made him feel the things he'd felt when he'd kissed her. He'd never felt lightning before, never had his knees go weak.

But she was right about one thing. The truce was over. The war was on. And Maggie Hazelwood Randolph was both the enemy and the prize—the prize he intended to win.

He turned from watching her disappear into the kitchen and searched the crowd across the room. There. "Noah!" he shouted.

At Alex's signal, Noah rose from his booth and started winding his way toward the center of the room. Alex met him halfway and slung an arm around the man's shoulders.

"Noah, my man, let's talk. I've got a proposition for you."

* * *

By the time she got home that night, Maggie was so utterly exhausted she could barely climb the stairs to her room. Noah had brought the kids home around ten, and they and he were sound asleep, a condition Maggie intended to personally indulge in as soon as she hit the bed.

But it didn't happen. The instant she closed her eyes she saw Alex's lips reaching for hers, felt his breath on her cheek, his hands on her shoulders.

Oh, Lord, why did it have to be him? Why did the first man she'd kissed in six years have to be a damn bull rider? And why, heaven help her, did the kiss have to make her feel . . . so much?

She tried to shove the feelings aside, the heat, the longing, the *rightness* of his lips on hers, but they wouldn't be shoved. Her heartbeat wouldn't be slowed. The terrible yearning for another taste wouldn't be stilled.

Damn the man.

She didn't want to feel these things. She and her life had been perfectly fine until he came along. She wanted her life back to its safe, predictable routine. Dull, maybe, but safe.

Alex Dillon was anything but safe.

How would she face him in the morning after a kiss like that? How would she face herself?

She faced herself the next morning the same way she did every morning—head on and full speed, without leaving much time for soul searching.

As for Alex, she didn't have to face him at all. He didn't come to the café for breakfast.

Good. Something was going her way for a change. Maybe she could make it through the entire day without seeing him. If he didn't come in for lunch, and she didn't look out her kitchen window when he came to exercise his horse, she would consider herself lucky.

She wasn't lucky.

Halfway up her driveway that afternoon she slammed on the brakes and skidded to a stop. She simply could not, would not, believe what she saw. That could not be a travel trailer parked along the near side of the cedar windbreak just east of the barn. It could not be the same travel trailer she'd seen parked behind the feed store since a certain man had come to town. That could not be the same shiny black pickup parked next to the trailer that she was used to seeing around six-thirty every evening.

And that certainly could not be Noah Eugene Randolph helping Alex Dillon hook up the old TV antenna, the one that had been stored in the garage for years, to that trailer.

She blinked, but the nightmarish apparition did not disappear. She prayed, but it didn't disappear. She cursed, she pounded on the steering wheel, and she ground her teeth. Alex Dillon and his travel trailer were still there, parked, hooked up, and settled in, not two hundred feet from her back door.

Maggie slapped her foot on the accelerator and barreled up to her parking spot in front of the garage. When she got out, she slammed the door so hard the van rocked on its wheels.

Calm. She had to remain calm. She would not rush over to that trailer and start screaming like a banshee. She wouldn't.

With her purse tucked up under one arm, Maggie marched across the packed dirt. Alex climbed down from the roof of the trailer and stood beside Noah, waiting for her.

Imagine that idiot crawling around up there like a

monkey. Wasn't he satisfied to fall off bulls? He had to try trailers, too?

They stood there, the two of them, staring her down defiantly. With every step she took, she stared right back.

"What the hell do you think you're doing?" Good grief. She was screaming. Like a banshee.

Both men blinked, then glanced at each other.

Noah cleared his throat. "I've rented Dillon a little space for his trailer. He'll be living out here."

"Oh, he will, will he?"

"Well, I offered him the spare bedroom upstairs, but he turned me down."

"You off—" Maggie clamped her mouth shut. She would not stand out here in the wind, with rain on the way, and argue with two mule-headed cowboys.

She gave Noah a long look, then turned her gaze on Alex. It was a mistake. The look he gave back was bold, too bold. She read laughter in his dark brown eyes. Laughter, and challenge. Maggie fought to keep her expression blank, when those eyes of his were sending messages to parts of her body that had no business receiving messages from a man like him. From any man, for that matter.

Without a word or nod, she turned and marched to the house. She spent the rest of her afternoon and evening fighting the urge to throw things and slam doors. When Noah came in, she refused to talk about Alex. He didn't push the subject, but the kids were another story. Maggie thought she'd never get through their excited talk at dinner about having Alex living right outside their back door.

After dinner she helped Doug with his math and supervised Cindy's coloring in her coloring book. Then came a little TV, followed by baths, followed by bed.

By the time they were asleep, even Noah had turned in for the night.

"Must have worn himself out helping our new tenant move in," she muttered with disgust.

Okay. The house was quiet, everyone was in bed, and Maggie finally had the privacy she desperately needed. Privacy to pace the floor and think.

Why had Alex moved his trailer here? Why had Noah let him, invited him? And the big question—what was she going to do about it?

She knew she had to do something. After the way he'd kissed her last night, the way she had responded, she knew for her own sake she needed to stay as far away from Alex as she could get.

At the end of the den she turned and paced back toward the kitchen. On her way past the coffee table, she picked up a stray crayon Cindy had left. A few paces later Maggie dropped it into the junk drawer at the end of the kitchen counter.

Alex had to go. She would not have a bull rider living practically on top of her. What stunned her and hurt to admit was that she was attracted to him. She, Maggie Randolph, was attracted to a rodeo bull rider.

She shook her head and paced another lap through the den and back. He had to leave. He couldn't stay where he was. She couldn't spend her days and nights with him so close, worrying about running into him every time she stuck her nose out the door. It would never work.

When she reached the end of the kitchen again, she glanced out the window into the yard. The yard light atop the utility pole cast a greenish hue over the not-quite-so-green lawn and the packed red earth that stretched from the end of the yard to the barn. To Alex's trailer.

His light was on.

Before she could talk herself out of it, Maggie opened the back door and stepped onto the porch. The rain had missed them, but the night was still cloudy. Warm, humid wind swept in from the south. Other than that, the only sound to be heard was a diehard cricket underneath the back porch that didn't know it was November.

Maggie took a deep breath, for strength, for calm, and left the porch. She walked slowly, straight for the little trailer. She wiped her palms on the thighs of her jeans, then knocked on Alex's door.

She heard a thump that seemed to shake the trailer, then footsteps. The instant Alex opened the door, she knew she'd made a mistake in coming. How was she supposed to talk to a man who wore a pair of jeans, a surprised look, and nothing else?

His bare feet were long and narrow, with well-shaped toes. His bare chest was . . . the word that came to mind was *magnificent*. Muscles that looked rock-hard formed mounds and valleys that tapered down his chest to a flat, ridged stomach, and it was all covered in sleek, smooth-looking bronze skin. Smooth. Hairless. She'd never seen a man with a hairless chest before. Not face to face. Or, face to chest, as it were.

But there was hair on him. It started just below his navel and disappeared beneath the waistband of his low-riding jeans.

Her mouth went dry. She tried to swallow.

Suddenly Alex jerked. He stepped sideways and reached beyond her line of sight, then came back and slipped on a shirt. "Hi. I wasn't expecting you."

He'd been half naked but not expecting her? *Well, that's a relief.* He still hadn't buttoned his shirt.

She shouldn't have come. But she was here, so she might as well do what she had set out to do, say what needed to be said. "I . . . I'd like to talk to you."

"Sure. Come on in."

He stepped back, but not enough for her peace of mind. She had to squeeze past him, brushing much too close to that strip of smooth, bare flesh revealed by his unbuttoned shirt. Close enough to be warmed by his heat, to feel his breath on her forehead. Close enough to make her breath catch and her heart pound.

Then she was past him and inside, but it was still too close. The interior of the trailer couldn't have been more than seven feet wide. She moved another step away from him, which put her leg up against a coffee table.

The inside of the trailer surprised her. The outside was faded by the sun and pitted here and there by road gravel, with several small dents scattered about for good measure. She had expected, much to her own private embarrassment, for the inside to be somewhat shabby. At least messy. It was neither.

Alex's tiny home on wheels was as clean and neat as the formal living room of the most fastidious homemaker. Certainly it was cleaner and neater than her own house.

To her right, against the front wall, a brown sofa stretched from one side wall to the other. Over each arm, a small wall-mounted lamp cast a circle of golden light onto the sofa cushions. In the daytime, the big front window would provide plenty of light.

Before the sofa sat the coffee table Maggie stood next to. It held a paperback copy of a—good grief, was that a Janet Dailey book? It was! One of her Calder series.

Well, well, well. The man's taste was not all in his

mouth after all. Of course, the book was about cowboys and ranches, so she guessed it maybe wasn't all that strange that Alex was reading it. Maybe no one had told him it was a romance novel.

Next to the open paperback stood a soft drink can, on a coaster, no less.

Behind her, next to the front door, a brown and black plaid wingback chair took up the space from the couch to the door. The opposite wall bore a built-in, waist-high cabinet, on which rested a small portable television.

Next came a full, but minuscule kitchen, surely smaller than the one she'd had in the backyard playhouse her father had built her for her seventh birthday. The ceiling light provided most of the light for the living room as well as the kitchen.

A short counter, just long enough to accommodate two bar stools, extended as a divider between kitchen and living room.

Beyond the kitchen she caught a glimpse of what must have been the bathroom door. The bedroom took up the back end of the trailer. She couldn't see into it but imagined it barely large enough for a double-sized bed, if that.

Every surface she saw was spotless and spoke of care. There weren't even any dirty dishes on the kitchen counter.

What a strange man.

Behind her, Alex closed the front door. "Have a seat." He nodded toward his soft drink. "Can I get you one of those?"

"Oh. No, thanks." She sat on the wingback chair. When he plopped down onto the end of the sofa—the end nearest her—she tried not to stare at the way the kitchen light gleamed off that bare strip of chest and highlighted the planes and angles formed by firm, hard muscles. "I, uh, it looks like I've interrupted your reading."

Alex glanced at the book on the coffee table, then raised his dark eyes slowly, deliberately up her body until he met her gaze. "Is that what you wanted to talk to me about? My reading?"

His gravelly voice was deep and quiet. And challenging. It sent goose bumps down Maggie's backbone. She suppressed a shiver. "No," she said. "I want to ask you a question."

"Go right ahead."

She held his gaze a long moment, then asked, "Why are you here?"

He grinned. "In your backyard, you mean?"

"That's right."

"So I can spend more time working with Cody."

"I don't see how having your trailer here makes a difference. You still have to be at the feed store all day, don't you?"

"Yeah," he said. "But this way I'll be around Saturday afternoons and all day Sundays. If I want to stop working him and get something to eat, I don't have to drive back into town. I can just walk across the yard."

"Just why does this horse of yours need so much work?"

Alex shrugged. "He's a cutting horse. A *top* cutting horse. I need to keep him in shape, keep him sharp, so we can enter the futurity next year."

"I thought you were a bull rider."

"I am. But that's not all I am, Maggie."

There it was again, that low, intimate tone in his voice. Maggie resisted its pull. "Well, how long do you plan to be around?"

He grinned again. "If I didn't know better, I'd think you were trying to get rid of me."

"You don't know better," she shot back. "How long, Alex?"

"Well, let's see." He arched his neck and gave the ceiling a thoughtful look. "I promised Clint I'd manage the store for as long as he needed me. He just got elected to a two-year term as state representative. His term doesn't start until January. I guess," he said, meeting her gaze with a cocky grin, "I'll be around for just over two years."

Maggie stiffened. "Not here!" she cried.

Alex gave her an exaggerated look of innocence. "Where else am I supposed to live? In case you haven't noticed, there's no such thing as an apartment complex in Deep Fork, and you can't really expect me to spend two years living in back of the feed store. Surely you're not *that* cruel."

"Oh, give me a break, Alex." Then she shrugged. "I really don't care where you live, but I came here to ask you a favor."

"A favor? Favors are usually asked between friends. Does this mean we're friends?"

Maggie folded her hands in her lap and studied them. He wasn't making any of this easy. She chose to ignore his question. "I came to ask you to leave, Alex." She met his gaze again. "To load up your horse, pack up your trailer, and leave."

With smooth, graceful movements, Alex leaned back against the cushion and propped his bare feet on the coffee table right next to her knees. Without taking his eyes off her, he clasped his hands behind his head, elbows extended, and asked softly, curiously, "Why?"

"Because I'm asking you to. Because you and your horse are disrupting our lives. My children are frightened of horses. Maybe that's my doing, maybe it's not, but I won't have you criticizing me for how I raise my family."

Alex lowered his arms. "Who am I to criticize how a mother raises her kids?"

"You were certainly doing a fine job of it the other day."

"I wasn't criticizing, not really."

"Could have fooled me."

"I just wanted you to realize that caution, skill, and respect for danger are better things, more useful things to teach a kid than fear. Fear cripples, Maggie."

He lowered his feet to the floor and leaned forward. "Besides, you and I are both wrong on this one. I've seen the way your kids look at Cody, and believe me, it's not with fear. Those kids aren't one bit afraid of him."

Maggie stiffened. He couldn't be right. She didn't want him to be right. He was making it up, just to get to her. "It doesn't matter. I'll never allow them near anything that has to do with rodeos."

Alex leaned closer, so close she could feel his breath stirring the hair at her temple. "Come on, Maggie, tell the truth. Your wanting me to leave doesn't have anything to do with horses or your fear for your kids or your fear of the rodeo."

"Then what," she said with an arched brow, "does it have to do with?"

"It has to do with you and me, and last night, when I kissed you."

A hot shiver broke loose down her spine. "It most certainly does not!"

Her words came out so fast, so hot, so defensive sounding, even Maggie recognized the false ring they carried. Alex most certainly did. He leaned even closer. "Liar."

This time there was no easy, exploratory touch of lip on lip. Alex slipped off the couch onto his knees beside her chair and his mouth took hers instantly, fully, fiercely.

Maggie froze, not daring to even breathe. This was not what she had come for. She didn't want this. *She didn't*.

Then his mouth moved and his tongue traced the seam of her lips. She tried to keep her lips sealed, she really did. But how could she when fireworks shot off behind her eyelids and heat pooled low in her belly?

She parted her lips.

Alex groaned and slipped his tongue inside. His arms encircled her and pulled her flush against the arm of the chair, which was all that separated them.

He buried his hands in her hair. Maggie moaned. How long had it been since she'd felt strong masculine fingers in her hair, on her scalp? A lifetime. A long, lonely lifetime. She wrapped her arms around his back and held on tight. He felt so warm and solid beneath her hands. She yearned to feel his bare skin beneath her fingers.

This shouldn't be happening, not with this man. But it was, and for the life of her, Maggie couldn't bring herself to pull away. Not when their mouths fit so perfectly, not when his hands, one still in her hair, the other feverishly roaming her back, felt so warm, so right. Not when her breath caught and her heart pounded.

Oh, Alex, what are you doing to me?

She shivered in his arms.

He kissed his way down her chin and neck and whispered her name. "Maggie, Maggie, you don't have to be afraid of me. I'd never hurt you, Maggie, I swear."

At the sound of his voice, reality intruded. Alex's words were like a bucket of ice water in the face. Maggie stiffened and pulled back, eyes wide as she stared at him. "Hurt me?" she managed in a choked whisper. "You'll *destroy* me."

have fallen off and proved yourself right. Fearing some-

SIX

Alex braced his hands against the open doorway and watched Maggie flee across the hard-packed dirt, up the sidewalk to the porch steps. His muscles strained to go after her. The dark shadows of the covered porch swallowed her from sight. An instant later a rectangle of light flashed as Maggie opened the back door. It slammed shut behind her.

He'd never seen anyone move so fast as when Maggie had pushed away from him a moment ago and fled out his door.

With hands clenched around the door frame, he watched the house across the way, wondering why she had said that about his destroying her. The kitchen light went out. It was a long moment before an upstairs light came on. Her bedroom light.

He turned away from the sight. If he gave rein to thoughts of Maggie in her bedroom, undressing, stretching out between crisp sun-fresh sheets, all naked and soft and warm . . .

"Damnation."

He pushed his front door shut and leaned back against it, eyes closed. He wasn't surprised to find his heart still pounding. It hadn't slowed yet from kissing her. Thinking of her in her bedroom would send it pounding right out of his chest.

With a frustrated oath, Alex flicked off the lights in the living room and kitchen. The trailer filled with the greenish glow from the yard light outside.

He could still taste her on his lips and tongue, could still feel her breath on his face, her hands on his back. God, what was happening to him? No woman had ever had this effect on him. He'd never known this driving need to just see a woman's smile, hear her laughter.

She had never smiled and laughed with him. Maybe never would, the way she felt about bull riders. And maybe she was right to feel that way. After what had happened to her husband right before her eyes, how could he ask her to get involved with him, when he had every intention of going back to the rodeo?

Or did he?

Alex threw himself down on his bed and wondered. Would he really go back to riding bulls? Did he have the nerve?

What he couldn't figure out was what, precisely, he was afraid of. Was it the risk of permanent injury? Or was it the mere thought of ending up mincemeat beneath the hooves of a two-thousand-pound Brahma?

He couldn't honestly say it was either of those. Those were merely the risks a man took when he climbed on top of a bull whose goal in life was to rid himself of the weight on his back. Alex was used to those risks, had lived with them for years.

The thing that kept coming back to his mind was that he was most afraid of . . . of being afraid.

"Now that makes sense, you idiot," he said into the semidarkness.

No, it didn't make any sense, but he understood it. He understood the legacy his father had left him.

The man had left Alex with the blood of his Sac and Fox and Kickapoo ancestors but no feeling of any tribal heritage, a love of rodeoing, and a knack with horses. And fear.

Alex had been too young to understand where his father's fear had come from, what had caused it. All he knew was that one day his father was too afraid to ride the bulls anymore. And the man's fear had left him ashamed.

That was what Alex feared. He feared one day not being able to ride. He feared not being able to face himself.

Lee Dillon hadn't been able to face himself, much less his family and friends. He'd lost himself in the bottom of a bottle and disappeared, leaving a wife and son alone and scared and bewildered.

Alex wondered where his old man had ended up. If he was even still alive.

A heck of a thing when a son didn't know if his own father was still alive.

A heck of a thing when a man didn't understand his own fear.

A heck of a thing when a woman could make a man question his life, his future.

Because, he suddenly realized, he had no future. Not the way things stood. He had a job that would last two years and would keep him off the major rodeo circuits. But what then? What did he have to offer a woman like Maggie Randolph?

If he did go back to bull riding, it was a simple fact

that he couldn't do it forever. Hell, at thirty-eight he was already considered over the hill for bull riding.

Just what was he going to do with the rest of his life?

He had money stashed away, sure. Enough to live on for a while, if he didn't develop champagne taste on what would have to be a beer budget. But a family costs money.

Family? Good God. He'd kissed her twice, and he was thinking in terms of *family?* Forget family. Maggie didn't even want his *horse* around, let alone him.

But even without a family, a man had to *do* something. He couldn't just lie around all day. He needed something to do, something with his hands and his mind, something worthwhile to give worth to his life. A man had to feel useful. Else, why hang around at all?

Why hang around at all?

With sudden clarity, Alex knew why his father had left. It wasn't just the fear, it was the uselessness he must have felt at not providing for his family. The rodeo money his father had won over the years hadn't been tremendous, but with his horse-training fees and what Alex's mother earned as a bank teller in Shawnee, the family had never really wanted for anything.

His father had felt he had no future, nothing to offer a wife and son. So he had left.

Would the same happen to Alex? When he couldn't ride bulls any longer, would he feel as if his life were over? Would he lose interest in everything else?

Would he start drinking? He shuddered.

No. He knew himself better than that. Alex learned a long time ago, out behind the feed store with Clint, that he couldn't hold his liquor. He got drunk too easily, got cranky, like a spoiled kid, then promptly got sick.

No. Alex wouldn't turn to drink.

So what *would* he do with the rest of his life?

It was barely light the next morning when Maggie heard the barn door creak open. Alex was up. Like a bee to nectar—or, she thought with despair, a fly to a spiderweb—she went to her bedroom window and looked out.

Cody stood saddled and ready. With arrogant ground-eating steps, Alex led him out of the corral and into the pasture. Once Alex had closed the gate, he swung up into the saddle, then leaned down and rubbed the animal's neck. Then he straightened. With a sharp shout and a jab to Cody's sides with the heels of his boots, Alex set the horse in motion.

As was the way with quarter horses, the muscles in Cody's hindquarters bunched, and in less than a heartbeat, he had gone from complete standstill to all out full gallop. Maggie had seen it all her life and never tired of the sight. Zero to sixty in two seconds, a car salesman would boast.

Cody's smooth chestnut coat gleamed in the predawn light. Alex rode in the saddle with skill and ease, as though he'd been born there. Man and horse were one as they streaked across the morning. The sight was beautiful. Stirring. And as she watched, fear was the farthest thing from Maggie's heart.

How long had she been kidding herself? It was so clear just then, standing in the murky light watching man and horse disappear over the rise. She wasn't the least bit afraid of horses. Never had been.

She wondered what Alex would say to that. She wondered what he'd say if he ran across her saddle tucked away in a blanket, in a box, on a high shelf in the tack room. He'd know instantly it was hers—it had her initials hand-tooled into the leather skirt.

Not having thought of the saddle in years, Maggie smiled with the memory. Steve had special-ordered it from a local saddlery for their first wedding anniversary. It had been quite a family joke for years, because that particular anniversary, Maggie had been eight months pregnant with Stephen. She hadn't been able to even *see* her feet, let alone lift one to the stirrup and swing up onto a horse.

But after she had recovered from Stephen's birth, the beautiful custom-made saddle had been waiting for her. She'd spent so many hours in it over the next five years, it probably even now wouldn't hold anyone else's shape but hers.

The memories the saddle brought were sweet ones.

Noah was right. It was time to let go of her anger. Past time.

But she had nursed it, fed it, lived with it for so long, what would be left if she let it go? What would be left of Steve?

A shaft of sunlight shot over the horizon and pierced the sky. And with it came a sudden clarity. She wasn't using her anger to hold on to Steve, as she had secretly believed. Steve had his own special place in her heart where he would always live, and he lived every day in each of his children, in Noah.

No, Maggie wasn't using her anger to hold on to him. She squeezed her eyes shut in shame. *I've been using it to punish him, to blame him for dying when I needed him here with me.*

If she used her anger to keep her children from doing the things Steve had loved, she could, God help her, say to Steve, "See? See what your bull riding, when you knew I didn't want you to do it, is making me do to your children?"

Oh my God. Her throat closed up and the backs of her eyes stung fiercely. "Steve, I'm so sorry. Please forgive me."

And there, alone in her room at dawn, she let go of her anger. And she cried.

She cried for Steve, for a life cut short; for her children, for the self-serving restrictions she had placed on their lives; she cried for Noah, who had put up with her anger for so long. She cried for herself.

At that last realization, she dried her eyes. There was no need to cry for herself. Sure, she missed Steve. He was her first, her one and only love, the father of her children.

But she had her children, her bright, beautiful, healthy children, and she had Noah.

What about Alex? a tiny voice asked.

Nothing about Alex, that's what. Maybe she *was* finally getting her head on straight, but that didn't mean she would ever fall for a man who made a living out of what killed Steve. No way.

But as the room lightened, so did Maggie's spirits. If she could respond to Alex, a man whose very way of life she opposed, then surely, *surely* she could find another man out there in the world if she wanted to. A man who could make her feel those things she had unwillingly felt in Alex's arms the two times he had kissed her. A safe, sane man. Maybe a banker or a plumber. A safe, sane man who didn't ride bulls but who could make her blood sizzle with a mere look.

Yes. She could fall for a man like that—if she decided she wanted a man in her life, which she didn't.

By the time she showered and dressed and made her way downstairs, Noah was already halfway through a pot of coffee. Before pouring herself a cup, she went to Noah where he sat at the kitchen table. She put her arm around him and kissed the top of his head, ignoring the taste of his hair oil. "I love you, Noah Randolph."

Noah craned his neck around and looked at her. "Well, I love you, too, Maggie girl."

"No," Maggie said, "I mean I really love you. I'm not sure how, or even why, you've put up with me all these years, but I thank you for it. I think you'll find life a little easier around here from now on."

Alert, Noah watched her as she eased her hug. A curious gleam came to his eye. "How's that?"

Maggie released him and straightened. "I've finally taken your advice." She looked him in the eye. "I'm not angry anymore, Noah. I've let it go."

Noah's blue eyes filled swiftly. With a loud throat clearing, he turned and took a slow sip of coffee, then carefully set the mug down again. "Well." He cleared his throat again. "Well, that's just fine. Just fine, Maggie girl."

Maggie sniffed back her own tears while Noah tried to hide that he used his sleeve to wipe his face. She took her time pouring her own cup of coffee, then sat across the table from him.

"So," he said more forcefully than necessary. "Looks like it's going to be a real beauty of a day out there."

When he looked at her, his grin was slow and full. So was Maggie's. "Yes," she told him. "It's going to be a real beauty."

Maggie breezed through her hours at work with a smile. When she got home that afternoon, she found Noah draped over the fender of his old pickup, hidden from the waist up by the raised hood. She laughed out loud. He looked like Jonah being swallowed by the whale. The pickup looked fully prepared to close its jaws over him any instant.

A once-red shop rag, now covered in grease, hung limply from Noah's hip pocket. Each occasional clank of metal against metal from under the hood was followed by a sharp curse.

"Trouble?" she asked.

"Ah, dangit." He pulled himself from beneath the hood and straightened, holding some obviously troubled part of the pickup in a hand covered with more grease than the rag in his pocket. "Dang alternator quit chargin' on me."

"That's an alternator, huh?"

He turned the thing in his hand. "That's a dead alternator. Gonna need to borrow your van and see if I can find a replacement in town. Might have to go to Shawnee to get one, but I'll try Jacktown Salvage first."

"Sure." She pulled her keys out of her purse. "Here you go." She held them out to him.

He reached to take them, then jerked his grimy hand back and wiped it on his overalls. "Maybe I better clean up a little first."

Maggie grinned. "I was hoping you'd at least take that rag out of your pocket before you sat in my clean van."

Noah laid the alternator on the radiator and followed Maggie to the house. After he washed up at the sink in the combination mud and laundry room just inside the back door, he took Maggie's keys and headed out.

"Oh, Noah," she called. "I forgot to get chicken scratch on the way home, and we're out. Can you pick up a bag?"

From where he had stopped just beyond the porch

steps, Noah gave her a considering look. "Forgot, huh?"

Maggie shifted uncomfortably.

The look he gave her said he knew better. He could see right through her and knew exactly why she had "forgotten" to stop at the feed store.

She straightened her shoulders. Just because she had decided to let go of her anger didn't mean she had any intentions of getting involved with another damned bull rider. She got enough of Alex Dillon right on her own doorstep. Could she help it if she was reluctant to put herself in his company any more often than absolutely necessary?

"Yes," she told Noah. "I forgot."

With a smirk and a wave, he headed across the yard. "I'll get your scratch, Maggie girl. I'll get it."

Not long after he left, Maggie heard the school bus stop down at the end of the driveway. Minutes later the house filled with the sound of active children. They whizzed in, changed into play clothes, and whizzed back out to play. Now that the days were getting so short, they had to get their playing done in a hurry. Homework could always wait until after dark.

Maggie had just put in a load of laundry when she heard the scream from the front yard. Not a playful shriek followed by laughter, nor a cry of indignation followed by heated voices. This was a scream. More than one. As Maggie froze for an instant, she heard fear, and from another young voice, excruciating pain.

She shot out of the house at a dead run. Where? Where were they?

Another cry.

There! Beneath the maple.

Breathless, her heart pounding somewhere near her

throat, Maggie ran for all she was worth. Terror tasted like copper in her mouth.

The three children huddled beneath the tree.

"What happened?" Maggie cried, still a dozen yards away.

"Mommy, Mommy!" Cindy leaped from Doug's side and ran for Maggie, tears streaming down her tiny face. "Dougie fell out of the tree!"

Oh, God, oh, God. Please let him be all right.

Maggie scooped Cindy up by the waist with one arm without slowing her pace. When she reached the boys, she lowered Cindy to the ground and crouched beside a writhing Doug. He was holding his arm against his chest and crying.

Maggie felt ice creep into her veins. Doug was not a crier. She took a deep breath and tried for calm. "Let me see, honey."

"It hurts, Mom."

"I know. Let me see."

"It's his wrist," Stephen said, eyes wide. "He fell out of the tree and landed on it. I think he broke it, Mom."

Maggie quailed. As a mother, she'd been lucky. She'd never had to deal with a broken bone before. Not on one of her children. One of her babies.

"Come on, honey, let's get you to the house and take a look." She helped Doug to his feet. He cried out once, sending a stab of pain and fear into Maggie's gut.

When they made it to the kitchen, she finally got Doug to let go of his arm and lower it to the table. He could move his fingers, but barely, and not without moaning.

Maggie tried to be as gentle as possible while wrapping a towel around his arm from his elbow down, but it was hard with the way her hands were shaking.

"Get in the freezer and bring me three bags of frozen peas," she told Stephen.

While waiting for the peas, Maggie stroked the hair back from Doug's face. His tears were drying, but his face was still white. "I know it hurts, honey, but we'll fix it, I promise."

"Is it broke, do you think?" he asked.

"I don't know, honey." He needed X-rays. And she had no way to get to town!

Noah. She had to find Noah.

Stephen brought the bags of peas, and Maggie packed them gently over Doug's arm. She told him to be still, then she grabbed the phone. Maybe Noah had stopped at the feed store first. Maybe he was still there.

Alex answered. Noah had been and gone. Maggie swore.

"Maggie? What's wrong?"

She took another deep breath. "I think Doug just broke his wrist, Noah's got my van, and the pickup won't run."

"I'll be right there."

Before Maggie could answer, nothing but a dial tone remained on the line. She sagged with relief. Alex was coming. Alex would help her.

Alex called Jeff Bonner, his afternoon help, from the warehouse. "Here's the keys. You're on your own, kid. Lock up at six and take the keys over to the café. I'll get them in the morning. If you think you need help, call Tom."

Without waiting for an answer, Alex sprinted for his pickup and headed for the river. He had only one thing on his mind. He had to get to Maggie. Maggie needed him.

Little boys took tumbles all the time. Though Alex didn't like to think of one of Maggie's kids in pain, he knew they were tougher than Maggie realized.

Then again, how tough could they be, having been protected by Maggie all their lives, kept from anything she deemed harmful? When it came to that, Alex wondered what Doug had been doing that could have resulted in a broken wrist. Heaven knew those kids weren't allowed to do anything "dangerous."

But remembering his own childhood, Alex knew kids could get hurt just tripping over their own feet.

No matter how it had happened, from the sound of Maggie's voice, she wasn't taking it very well. She needed him.

Once across the bridge he took the road to Maggie's as fast as his tires could spit gravel. At the house, he ignored the concrete parking slab, the sidewalk, the lawn. He pulled up right next to the back steps.

Little Cindy, eyes wide, face pale, met him at the back door.

"Where's your momma and Doug?"

"In the kitchen. Dougie fell out of the tree and got hurt."

Tree? Maggie actually lets her kids climb trees? Well, he'd bet his last dollar *that* particular form of recreation would come to a screeching halt after this.

He found them at the kitchen table, Maggie kneeling beside Doug, fussing over him, Stephen watching solemnly.

Maggie looked up at him, eyes huge and haunted in her pale face. "Thanks for coming, Alex."

He shrugged. "Let's have a look," he said.

He was pleased to notice Maggie's hands barely

shook at all when she removed the bags of—frozen peas? They were. Frozen peas. Heck of a deal, but they made perfect ice packs.

"Does it still hurt?" he asked Doug.

The boy sniffed. Tear tracks streaked his cheeks. "Not really. Now it's just cold."

Alex nodded. "You tell me if I hurt you."

Doug sniffed again, then nodded, bracing himself for whatever Alex had in mind. The trust in the boy's eyes humbled him.

Alex gently felt the wrist and lower arm, and Doug didn't flinch. Alex didn't want to bend the wrist in case it really was broken, but the injury didn't seem serious.

"Can you wiggle your fingers?"

Doug looked to Maggie.

"Give it a try, but be easy," Maggie said.

Doug carefully moved his fingers.

"Good," Alex said. "That's good. Looks like just a bad sprain to me, but we ought to get it X-rayed, just to be safe."

Maggie looked up at him again, and he felt himself falling into those huge green eyes.

"You really don't think it's broken?"

"No."

"You would know?"

Alex shrugged. "I've broken more than my share of bones. Come on. Let's get this fella to the nearest X-ray machine."

Maggie rose. "That'll be Shawnee. Dr. Palmer and his wife were in the café this morning, on their way to a camping trip, so his office in town is closed."

"Then we'll go to Shawnee."

"You're sure you don't mind? What about the store?"

"Don't worry about the store. Now let's do something with this boy's arm."

Alex helped Maggie fashion a sling using a large dish towel. They lined the sling with two bags of frozen peas, then as gently as possible, placed Doug's injured arm on top of the peas. More peas covered his arm, leaving it packed in ice.

Alex fought a grin when Doug refused to sit on Maggie's lap for the twenty-minute ride to Shawnee. Cindy ended up on Maggie's lap, with Doug and Stephen sandwiched in between Maggie and Alex.

Alex took the gravel road to the highway as carefully as he could to avoid jarring Doug's arm. Once on the blacktop he was able to speed up. He drove to the emergency entrance at Shawnee Hospital. He and Stephen and Cindy had to wait while Maggie went with Doug for his X-rays.

When Alex sat on one of the utilitarian sofas, Cindy climbed up in his lap. Funny what a six-year-old on his lap could do to a man's heart. If he had thought about such an occurrence, he would have thought he would feel awkward. After all, he'd never had a kid on his lap before.

But awkward was the farthest thing from how he felt with Cindy and her big green eyes. Warm was more like it.

"Will Dougie have to get a cast, Mr. Alex? Marylou Barnes broke her arm at school and she had to have a cast. We all got to draw on it."

"We'll just have to see, hon."

She looked over at Stephen, who stood at Alex's knee. "Are we gonna get in trouble for climbing the tree?"

Stephen grimaced. "Probably."

"Not allowed to climb trees, huh?" Alex asked.

Stephen hung his head. "No, sir."

"Sir? I thought Cindy told you, my name is Alex."

Stephen gave him a small smile, then sat next to him on the couch. For the next hour, both kids amazed Alex by how calm they stayed. No bickering and very little fidgeting. But Alex was still relieved when Maggie and Doug came down the hall.

Stephen and Cindy ran to Doug. Cindy looked disappointed. "You didn't get a cast."

Doug puffed out his chest and wagged his new regulation hospital sling, showing off his brand new Ace bandage. " 'Course not. It's only a sprain."

Maggie smiled up at Alex. "You were right. It wasn't broken."

Her smile did funny things to his heartbeat. Had she ever smiled directly at him before? "I'm glad." He looked at Doug. "You were lucky, kid."

Doug grimaced. "Yeah, that's what the doctor said."

Maggie arched a brow and took in all three of her children. "We'll talk about how lucky you're not going to be for the next few weeks after we get home."

"Aw, Mom," Doug complained.

"Don't give me any 'Aw, Mom,' or I'll forget all about the doctor's instructions."

"But you can't," Doug cried. "He said it was just the medicine I needed."

Maggie rolled her eyes. "I ought to make him pay for it."

"What medicine is it?" Alex asked.

Maggie sighed. "You didn't know what you were getting yourself into when you came to our rescue. That . . . doctor prescribed ice cream."

"Double dip chocolate on a sugar cone," Doug reminded her.

Alex bit the inside of his jaw to keep from laughing. "Double dip chocolate. Pretty strong medicine," he said to Doug. "Are you sure you're up to it?"

The boy grinned. "I'm tough. I can take it like a man."

That time Alex did laugh. "Come on then." He started herding them all toward the door. "I think we all could use a dose."

SEVEN

Because the kids hadn't had supper, Maggie decided they would all have a hamburger before the ice cream. She wanted to murder that doctor for prescribing ice cream in front of Doug. Sure, Doug had paid in pain for climbing a tree when he knew he wasn't supposed to. But the ice cream reeked too much of reward to suit Maggie.

Still, what could she do?

They stopped at Braum's on Kickapoo and MacArthur for burgers and ice cream. While waiting for their order, Maggie called home. Noah answered, and she explained what had happened.

"But he's okay?" Noah asked.

"He's okay. The doctor gave him something for the pain, something mild, he said. As soon as we eat and Doug gets his ice cream, we'll be home."

After reassuring Noah one more time, then another, that Doug was going to be fine, Maggie rejoined the others. A few minutes later their order was ready.

Maggie surreptitiously watched Alex throughout the

meal. She assumed, with his rodeoing life-style, that he hadn't been around children often, but he seemed to be holding his own. He talked and laughed easily and didn't bat an eye when Cindy smeared catsup on his cuff.

Maggie appreciated the way he did not talk down to the kids but treated them as real people.

He caught her eye now and then, and she glanced away each time quickly. Why, she didn't dare ask herself.

Doug had a time eating his hamburger with one hand, but he managed. He was still pale, but not as white as he had been when Maggie had first found him beneath the tree, crying and holding his wrist, eyes wide with fear and pain. She would remember that sight for the rest of her life. That, and the sound of screams.

Doug managed to make it all the way through his ice cream cone before his adrenaline ran out. In the pickup on the way home, still refusing to sit on Maggie's lap, he fell asleep with his head on her shoulder.

Alex glanced down at Doug, then up at Maggie. "I'd say he's had it for the day."

Maggie sighed. "I'd say we all have."

By the time they got home it was well past dark. Alex lifted Doug into his arms. The sight of Alex cradling one of her children against his chest squeezed at Maggie's heart. A warm aching yearning stole its way past her barriers.

Before they could climb out of the pickup, the back porch light flicked on and Noah came barreling out the back door.

Stephen leaned across Alex and yelled, "Grandpa, Doug's got a really neat bandage and sling. Wait'll you see."

Practically stumbling with exhaustion, Maggie followed Alex and the kids into the house. "I think it's time for these three to get to bed," she said.

Alex, with Doug still in his arms, headed for the stairs.

"Here," Maggie said, "I'll take him."

"I've got him. Just show me the way."

It was disconcerting, to say the least, watching Alex Dillon stride down her upstairs hall with one of her children in his arms. That yearning feeling came back, stronger this time than before. She tamped it down.

Alex lowered Doug to the bed, then, almost awkwardly it seemed, backed out of the room. Maggie smiled. Alex had been a godsend. The hours he had spent today with her and the kids couldn't have been easy for a footloose rodeo cowboy, but he hadn't seemed at all uncomfortable until he'd put Doug down.

It was only eight o'clock, but none of the kids objected to going to bed so early. Doug had roused briefly during the trip from the pickup to his bed, but he was asleep before Maggie pulled his covers up. Stephen and Cindy didn't last but a second or two past her goodnight kisses.

Maggie herself would have liked nothing better than to curl up in the dark, under the covers, and give in to her exhaustion, but she knew from experience she was too wound up to sleep. Then, too, Alex might still be downstairs, and she needed to thank him for what he'd done for her and her family.

He was still downstairs. She found him on the back porch with Noah, sipping coffee and enjoying the unseasonably warm evening. She poured herself a cup of coffee and joined them.

"Well," Noah said, "even though I wasn't here when all the excitement rolled through, I feel like I've had about enough for today myself. I'll be hittin' the hay now. Thanks again, Alex, for everything. I shoulda been here myself, but . . ."

"No problem," Alex said. "I was glad to be of service."

"I want Doug to stay home from school tomorrow," Maggie told Noah.

"Well, sure you do," Noah said. "Don't you worry. I'll look after him."

Maggie kissed his cheek. "I know you will."

Noah said his good nights again, then made his way back inside and to bed.

Maggie turned to Alex where he stood leaning one hip against the waist-high rail surrounding the porch. Light from the kitchen bathed one side of him in soft gold, while the yard light faintly washed the other half of him in a pale, ghostly green. "I'll add my thanks to Noah's. I don't know what we'd have done without you today."

"You're welcome," Alex said with a nod. Then he pointed with his chin toward the upstairs. "Everybody asleep up there?"

"Yeah." Maggie took a sip of her coffee. "They were beat."

"I think maybe you are, too. Why don't you sit down?"

The gravel in his voice was soft and low. For some inexplicable reason, Maggie's legs started trembling. Sitting down suddenly sounded like a good idea. She eyed the swing, then dismissed it. She would have to walk past Alex to get there. Then she would be in the dark corner, where the light didn't reach. What if he followed her, sat with her on that old swing?

Maggie turned away and sat on the middle step to the yard. She stared toward the barn and warmed her hands on the coffee cup. Her hands had turned to ice at the first scream that afternoon. She hadn't been warm since. "I can't do it, can I?"

"Do what?" Alex asked softly.

"Keep my children safe. Keep them from getting hurt."

Wooden boot heels echoed hollowly along the wooden porch until they stopped behind her. Clothing rustled, breath hissed, a knee cracked. And suddenly Alex was seated directly behind her on the top step, his big, battered boots planted one on each side of her on the step she occupied.

"Kids are kids, Maggie, and life is always full of booby traps. You know that. Today was just . . . life. That doesn't mean you're not doing a good job."

"But a tree." She shook her head. "They know they're not allowed to climb trees, and what happened this afternoon is exactly why they're not allowed."

"Hell, Maggie." Large warm hands touched her shoulders.

Maggie jumped.

"Easy. You're about as stiff as a fence post."

And then those hands, those . . . oh, those hands. They started a deep, hard massage on her shoulders that made Maggie want to weep with pleasure.

"Kids are going to have accidents, Maggie. This can't be the first time one of yours has been hurt."

"Of course not, but this is the worst."

"The worst?" The hands started down her back.

She arched like a cat stretching in the sun.

"Hell."

She could hear a smile in his voice.

"If this is the worst that's ever happened to any of your kids, you don't have anything to worry about. As long as you remember that forbidding a kid to do something—especially something all their friends probably get to do every day—is like waving a red flag in front of a bull."

"Please, let's don't talk about bulls."

The hands moved to her neck, her scalp. Ahhh.

"Right. No bulls. But trees, now, that's another subject. I assume you don't let them play in trees because you don't want them to get hurt."

"Of course. Why else would I tell them no?"

"You ever climb trees, Maggie?"

The hands felt strong and solid, and she felt her muscles unknot one by one. "Sure, I climbed my share when I was a kid. And before you ask, I also cussed, smoked a cigarette or two out behind the café—until Dad caught me—and rode horses."

The hands stilled. "Now that's interesting. Rode horses, huh?"

Why in the world had she told him that? She must be more tired than she knew to reveal something like that to him after their past discussions on the subject of horses.

"Bet you weren't any good at it," Alex said.

Maggie craned her neck and looked up at him. "Don't count on it, buster. I was damn good." *Now you've done it*.

He arched one brow and gave her a lopsided grin. "Why, Maggie Randolph, you're a fake."

"I am not." She faced forward again, hoping he'd resume the massage. "At the time, I had no idea how dangerous things like that were."

After a long pause, he started kneading her shoulders again. "Of course you didn't. And you shouldn't have. If every time you climbed up on a horse all you could think about was how dangerous it might be if you fell off, you'd never have been able to ride. You would have fallen off and proved yourself right. Fearing some-

THIS OFFICIAL ENTRY COULD WIN YOU A MILLION DOLLARS!
...or one of 1,254 All-Cash Prizes—Guaranteed To Be Awarded!
OFFICIAL PRIZE ROSTER

(1) GRAND PRIZE	(1) 1ST PRIZE	(1) 2ND PRIZE	(1) 3RD PRIZE	(1) 4TH PRIZE	1,250 5TH PRIZES
$1,000,000 ($25,000 a year for 40 years!)	**$25,000 CASH** ALL AT ONCE	**$15,000 CASH** ALL AT ONCE	**$10,000 CASH** ALL AT ONCE	**$5,000 CASH** ALL AT ONCE	**$20.00 CASH** (This is our very smallest prize!)

– DETACH AND MAIL CARD TODAY –

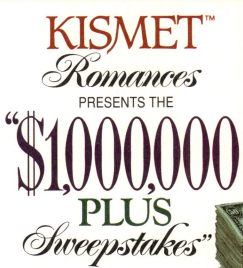

KISMET™
Romances
PRESENTS THE
"$1,000,000 PLUS *Sweepstakes*"

OFFICIAL ENTRY FORM

PLEASE PRINT CLEARLY

NAME _____

ADDRESS _____ APT _____

CITY _____ STATE ____ ZIP _____

PLEASE HELP! We need your opinion. Could you take a moment to answer just three questions listed below? Your cooperation will be greatly appreciated

1. How many Romance Books did you buy in the last 3 months? (Check One)
   ❏ None ❏ 1–3 ❏ 4–10 ❏ more than 10
2. How do you compare Kismet Romances to other romance lines? (Check One)
   ❏ Better ❏ Same ❏ Worse
3. Which influenced you to buy this Kismet Romance? (Check more than one if appropriate)
   ❏ Cover design ❏ Storyline ❏ Author ❏ Sweepstakes

© 1992 Meteor Publishing Corp.   RET001

AFFIX GOLD "YES!" COIN HERE

YES! Please enter me in the "$1,000,000+ Sweepstakes" (per the rules) and tell me if I'm a WINNER! **NO PURCHASE NECESSARY** See rules on inside back cover for alternate entry instructions

PLUS...
2nd Chance To Win GUARANTEE

You will automatically be entered in a drawing for all unclaimed prizes if not already a winner. (You could win $1 Million this way, so – be sure to mail in your Entry today)!

DETACH AND MAIL CARD TODAY–

FIRST CLASS MAIL

OFFICIAL ENTRY CARD

Kismet Romances
"$1,000,000+ Sweepstakes"
PO Box 7249
PHILA PA 19101-9895

PLACE POSTAGE STAMP HERE

thing—" His voice changed, sounded strained. His hands stilled again. "—can bring it about quicker than anything. Fear makes you clumsy, it distracts you from what you should be doing. It destroys your concentration, your confidence and, with them, your ability to do whatever it is you should be doing."

Maggie didn't want to hear about fear tonight, didn't want to think about it. Did he think she didn't understand? Did he think she didn't lie awake at night, even after all these years, wondering if her nagging, voicing her own fears to Steve, had gotten to him, had distracted or worried him to the point he couldn't hang on to that bull?

But no, she thought, Alex wasn't talking about her any longer. Something in his voice pulled her. She turned slowly toward him. He was staring off into the dark, a faraway look in his eyes. "What are *you* afraid of, Alex?"

He stared toward the pasture a long moment, then blinked and looked at her with another lopsided grin. "Right now?" His grin faded. He leaned closer and spoke softly. "Right now I'm afraid of leaving you here on this porch without kissing you."

Maggie sucked in a breath. Her heart skipped, her blood raced. "Alex, really."

He trailed a finger across her cheek. "You're supposed to say, 'Alex, really?' like a question. Then I can say, 'Yes, Maggie. Really.' "

She never knew, there on the steps in the half golden, half green light, just what made her do it, but she did. "Alex, *really?*"

Alex's eyes widened. He cupped her cheeks in his calloused palms and brushed his lips across hers.

Electricity. Sharp. Startling. Tingly.

"Yes, Maggie," he whispered against her mouth. *"Really."*

This time he kissed her with such gentleness she couldn't believe it. She hadn't expected that. As he tasted and nibbled and held her face as though it were a delicate flower he feared to crush, Maggie met a new side of Alex Dillon, one she hadn't believed he had. A soft side, tender and caring and nurturing.

Vulnerable.

The word whispered through her mind like the wind. Somehow, some way, this man was vulnerable.

Then he deepened the kiss, and all hint of vulnerability vanished. He became the conqueror, aggressive and sure of what he wanted, and he unleashed a fire inside her with his heat.

Emotions. So many, changing so fast. She couldn't grasp them long enough to name them, but they swamped her, and now she was the one who was vulnerable. But his arms came around her, cocooning her in warmth and safety. She had been so cold, so alone for so long, surely it was all right to accept this gift from him. He was so warm, so solid and alive, so real. Surely it was all right to be in his arms, to wrap her arms around him.

All right? It wasn't all right. It was . . . necessary. It was . . . inevitable.

And then, it was over. But he didn't let her go. He held her tightly and buried his face between her neck and shoulder. How had she ended up on his lap?

With his arms around her, he stroked her back. His hands were trembling.

Maggie pulled back and looked at him. His face looked drawn, strained by some unseen devil that plagued him. "Alex?"

He placed a soft, tender kiss on her forehead. "Go

inside, Maggie," he whispered roughly. "Before . . ." He closed his eyes and shook his head. "It's time for me to go."

He picked her up and put her on the step beside him, then stood. "Good night, Mag."

Maggie sat on the porch and watched him all the way across the yard until he disappeared inside his trailer.

She felt suddenly alone. More alone than she'd felt in ages. The only sounds in the night were the rustling of dead, brittle leaves on the blackjack oaks, and that lone, mixed-up cricket she'd heard the other night.

The cricket wasn't the only one mixed up. Something had happened between her and Alex tonight, something different, something . . . magical. Something scary.

Go inside, Maggie. Yes. She thought maybe she should do just that. She thought maybe she should have done it several minutes ago.

She rose to leave and nearly stumbled over their coffee cups sitting side by side just behind her. She hadn't even been aware of hers leaving her hand.

Alex stood under the cold shower and waited for the heat in his blood to cool. He hadn't meant to kiss her, had had no intention of doing it, no business doing it. But they'd been talking about fear, and that had raised all his questions about bull riding to the surface. Then a new fear had taken hold, a fear of life without Maggie. He hadn't been able to help but kiss her.

He shouldn't have done it, but because he had kissed her, he had learned something new about himself. Kissing Maggie gave him a thrill, a high he'd never felt before, not even on the back of a bull with the roar of a Sunday crowd in his ears and the eight-second buzzer telling him he'd made it.

Nothing in his life had ever come close to that before. Nothing, until Maggie.

And then came the questions. Did her kiss really excite him so much, or was he lying to himself, using Maggie as an excuse for saying he didn't want to ride bulls any longer?

He honestly didn't know. It was too confusing to think about.

But when his body cooled and his mind stayed hot with the memory of Maggie in his arms, he thought maybe, just maybe, what he felt for her was every bit as thrilling, as overwhelming, as real as he had believed.

Still, until he could answer his own questions, he had no business coming on to Maggie the way he'd been doing. He should have kept his hands to himself.

Easier said than done, when all he could think about was getting his hands, his lips back on her, touching her again, tasting her. He didn't think he would ever get enough of tasting her.

In light of his semi-determination to stay away from Maggie, going to the café for breakfast the next morning was not the most logical move Alex could have made, but he did it anyway. Well, he had to go to the café to get the keys to the store, didn't he?

Right.

He opened the door and stepped inside. The bell over his head jingled. A wave of music from the jukebox, The Judds, he thought, wailed past him.

And smells. They must do it on purpose, Alex thought. They probably had a fan in the kitchen to blow the smell of frying bacon and baking bread directly at the front door to stimulate the appetites of customers. It worked on him. Suddenly he was starving.

Across the room, Maggie looked up from where she was cleaning a table.

Their gazes met and locked. Alex's hunger turned from food to something else. She stood there with her wild red hair pulled back into a ponytail at her nape, with dirty dishes cradled in one arm, a wet dishrag dangling from the other hand, and Alex felt his heart pound. In her eyes he read the memory of the kiss they'd shared last night on her porch. She was thinking of it, remembering, as he was.

But damn. He couldn't tell how she felt about it. What was her mood today? Would she speak to him? How would she react? With anger again, now that the crisis with Doug was past? With indifference?

Alex pulled his hat off slowly, his gaze still on her, and offered her a smile.

A clatter in the kitchen drew her attention. She jerked her gaze from his, took a last swipe at the table with her rag, then hustled toward the swinging door in the back.

Alex took the booth next to the table Maggie had just cleaned and tossed his hat beside him on the vinyl seat. He wished he had a cigarette, but then, he didn't smoke. Never had. But just then it seemed like having a cigarette to play with would be a welcome distraction. The Judds gave up their slot on the jukebox to Clint Black. Alex bit the inside of his jaw and waited for Maggie to come out of the kitchen.

He didn't have to wait long. She came out only moments later and brought him water and coffee. But she didn't look at him, and he couldn't read her expression.

"Maggie?"

Her gaze raised slowly to meet his, then, with a slight blush that made his heart race, she smiled. "Hi."

He felt a tightness he hadn't been aware of ease in his chest. He returned her smile. " 'Mornin'."

Her smile widened. "You want the usual?"

I want . . . "Yeah, the usual."

By the time Alex finished eating, the jukebox had gone through Willie Nelson, Barbara Mandrell, The Oakridge Boys, Alabama, and The Nitty Gritty Dirt Band. Maggie rang out a customer, then headed Alex's way with the coffeepot. "I almost forgot to give you these." She handed him the keys to the feed store. "The note said Jeff Bonner left them here for you."

"Yeah, I told him to when I left the store yesterday. Thanks."

She hesitated a minute, as if she wanted to say something more, but instead, sighed and refilled his coffee cup. "Can I get you anything else?"

"No thanks. How's Doug this morning?"

Maggie shrugged one shoulder. "He was still asleep when I left, but that's usual. Noah will keep him home today."

Alex grinned. "I bet Doug won't like that."

Maggie cocked her head. "Why not? He's been known to invent excuses to stay home."

"Yeah, but not when he's got that neat bandage and a great war story to tell."

"I'll tell him a story, that's for sure, right across the seat of his pants if I ever catch him climbing a tree again."

"Ah," Alex said with a nod. "The operative word there is 'catch'. My guess is he'll confine his tree climbing in the future to when he knows you're not around."

Maggie's eyes narrowed.

"Hey," he said. "Boys are like that. What can I say?"

Maggie shook her head and picked up his empty plate. She made a move to leave, then stopped. "I'm fixing spaghetti tonight at the house. I thought, that is . . if you're not busy or anything, maybe you could . . . I mean, we'd like it if you could come to dinner. At seven. That is, if you . . . wanted to, I mean."

Well, I'll be damned. Stunned was too mild a word for what Alex felt. For a moment, all he could do was stare at her. Had she actually *meant* it? Maggie Randolph was inviting him to dinner? At her house? The funny thing was, she looked almost as surprised as he felt. Would she take it back?

"But if you'd rather not, I—"

"Seven?"

The uncertain look in her eyes touched him. "Yes."

"I'll be there."

"Oh," Stephen said looking up at her from the bottom of the stairs. "I thought we were having spaghetti. I guess we're going out instead."

Maggie felt heat sting her cheeks. She should have worn a T-shirt instead of the sequined sweater. She took the last two steps and brushed past Stephen. "You were right the first time. We're having spaghetti. We aren't going anywhere tonight."

In the kitchen she pushed her sleeves up and stood back as far as possible before taking the lid off the spaghetti sauce to give it a stir, trying to avoid splatters.

She tasted the sauce. Almost ready. By the time the spaghetti was done and the French bread was hot, the sauce should be perfect.

Was the sweater too much? Yes. If it made Stephen think they were going out, it was too much.

What had possessed her to invite Alex to dinner? He couldn't possibly have been any more stunned by her invitation than she had been. The words had just sort of formed all on their own, and before she knew it, they were out.

Dumb. Dumb, dumb, dumb.

She turned on the oven to preheat it, put a pot of water on to boil, then dashed back upstairs. The green silk blouse would be better. Not so fancy, but it matched her eyes and made her feel feminine.

But when she peeled the sweater off, she had to straighten her hair again. The brush kept slipping in her damp palm. She gripped it tighter. What was the matter with her? It was only Alex, for heaven's sake. It was only supper. No big deal.

With her hair finally brushed back into place and her green silk blouse tucked into the waistband of her winter-white slacks, Maggie turned to leave. She stopped halfway to the door and turned back. Just a tiny squirt of perfume. Nothing too obvious. No harm in it.

Back down in the kitchen, she took the arm-length roll of French bread from its foil wrapper and made an inch-deep slit in the top from end to end.

Noah came in and refilled his coffee cup. From the corner of her eye she saw him give her the once-over.

"Going out tonight?"

Maggie ground her teeth. Maybe it was the earrings. She never wore dangling earrings. But damn it, couldn't a woman dress up once in a while without being badgered about it? "No, we're not going out. Why do you ask?" *Oh, brilliant, Magoo. Left yourself wide open with that one, didn't you?*

She paused with the slicing knife in her hand and looked at Noah, practically daring him to say something.

He gave a small shrug. "No reason. Something sure smells good."

Maggie winced. "Is it too strong?"

Noah looked confused. "How can the smell of spaghetti sauce ever be too strong?"

She felt her cheeks sting again. She turned back to the counter, grabbed a handful of spaghetti, and dipped it into the pot of boiling water. As the submerged ends softened, she lowered the sticks until the boiling water swallowed them from her fingertips.

When she turned back around, Noah was gone.

She slathered butter into the cut on the bread, then sprinkled garlic powder over the butter and tucked the loaf back inside its foil wrapper.

The table. She hadn't set the table.

She supposed the dining room would be a bit too much for her family to handle. It wasn't, after all, a holiday. The kitchen table would have to do.

She wiped her palms on a dish towel—why wouldn't they stop sweating?—then grabbed a stack of plates from the cabinet and set it on the table. Like magic, but predictable as sunrise in the morning, Cindy appeared.

"Is it time?" Cindy asked.

"It's time." She bent and gave the child a hug. Cindy loved to help set the table.

"Ooo, Mommy, you smell good."

Maggie straightened and smiled. "You mean the sauce?"

"No." Cindy opened the flatware drawer and started counting out the forks. "Your 'fume. It smells pretty."

Maggie nearly groaned. Too much perfume. She knew it. She was making a fool out of herself.

When she realized what Cindy was doing, she said, "Set an extra place, honey. Alex is coming for dinner."

"Really? Mr. Alex is coming?"

Maggie caught herself just short of wiping her palms on her white slacks. "That's right," she told Cindy.

"How come?" Cindy asked.

Because your mother is an idiot, that's how come. "Because I invited him."

A prickling sensation struck the back of her neck. She turned swiftly and found Noah lounging in the doorway to the dining room, a grin of pure delight on his face.

"Well, I'll swan," he said. "I didn't know you had it in you, Maggie girl."

Doug pushed his way around Noah. "Alex is coming to dinner?"

"Is that why Mom keeps changing clothes every ten minutes?" Stephen asked from behind Noah's shoulder.

Then, as the perfect capper to the situation, the doorbell rang. Frantic, Maggie glanced at the clock. Seven. On the dot. Mr. Alex, it seemed, had arrived.

She whirled and stuffed the wrapped bread into the oven. "Noah, would you get the door, please?"

"You don't want to get it yourself?"

Her cheeks stung hotter than the blast from the oven. "I, uh, think I'll go up and . . . change clothes."

EIGHT

Maggie pressed icy damp palms to her fiery cheeks. Good grief. Why was she acting this way? With a soft curse, she unbuttoned the silk blouse and hung it back in the rear of her closet. The winter-white slacks went next to them, and the earrings went back into her jewelry box.

A deep breath. All I need is a deep breath. Then I'll be calm. Rational.

Although why she should become rational now, after a day of making a fool of herself, she had no idea.

Angry with her own behavior, Maggie slipped on a pair of clean pressed jeans, then fished a long-sleeved white cotton blouse from the closet. Plain, tailored, and sensible, but neat. It still wasn't her usual T-shirt, but at least it wasn't sequins or silk.

In the bathroom she removed her eye makeup and started over, this time with a lighter touch. On her way past the dresser, she curled her lip at the bottle of perfume. Then she took a deep breath, prayed for calm, and headed for the door.

He was down there, she knew. She could hear the deep gravel in his voice. Sweat popped out on her palms again. With a grimace, she wiped them on the thighs of her jeans.

Damn. What in the *world* had possessed her to invite him? He was going to think she was just another stupid female who didn't know her own mind. From the day he came to town she'd been telling him in no uncertain words she wanted nothing to do with him. Now she'd invited him to dinner.

Good grief.

"Anyway," Doug told Alex, "I get to go back to school tomorrow. Don't I, Mom?"

Maggie frowned. "Yes, you *get* to go back to school tomorrow."

She had to hand it to Alex. Doug habitually looked for excuses to stay home from school. Not that he wasn't a good student, he just seemed to be a little lazy now and then. And the excuses almost never worked. He rarely stayed home.

But Alex had convinced Doug everyone would want to see his new bandage, and Doug's eyes had lit at the thought of all that attention.

Maggie's only worry on the subject was she didn't care too much for glamorizing Doug's injury. She didn't want him to get the idea casts and bandages and crutches would amaze and impress his friends.

From across the table she caught Alex's gaze and forced herself to relax. How could he possibly know what ideas he might be sparking in Doug's devious little mind? Alex had gotten him excited about going to school, which was more than Maggie and Noah had managed.

Alex had done remarkably well all evening, in fact,

with regard to the children. He spoke with them easily and casually, just as he had the night before. And Alex and Noah got along as though they had known and respected each other for years.

Maggie's smile widened. Bless those two men. She could tell by the looks on their faces they wanted to talk rodeo, or at least horses, but those two words never came up all through dinner.

"Just watch out," Alex said to Doug. "You were lucky, falling out of that tree. You could just as easily have broken that wrist as sprained it."

"Yeah," Doug said, "but then I'd have a cast. That's better than a silly old bandage."

"If you think that sprain hurt yesterday, you'll be in for a big surprise if you ever do break something. There's nothing fun at all about a broken bone."

Maggie saw the gleam dim somewhat in Doug's eyes. *Thank you, Alex.*

"Besides," Alex said. "Once is okay, but if you start showing up every few months with a new cast, even a new bandage, instead of being impressed, your friends are going to start thinking you're a klutz."

The remaining sparkle in Doug's eyes vanished, and a thoughtful look came over him. *Oh, Alex, thank you.* "More coffee, Alex, Noah?"

Alex scooted his chair back. "I'll get it," he said. "You wait on people at work all day. No need to do it at home, too."

The ache in her tired feet eased a little, but a new one started somewhere in the region of her heart. She could get used to this man. She shouldn't, and she wouldn't, but she could.

"Anyway," Alex said from the coffeepot at the counter, "after a meal like that, I could use the exercise."

Maggie gave him a mock frown. "Are you saying my cooking is heavy?"

"Certainly not," he cried. He tossed Noah an exaggerated look of panic. "I'm saying your cooking's so good, I ate too much."

"Good job," Noah told him with a wink. "Got yourself out of that one real good, Dillon."

"You two," Maggie said, her mock frown still in place.

Alex and Noah both laughed.

When Alex filled her cup, then Noah's and his own, he returned to his seat. "No kidding, Maggie. This is one of the best meals I've ever had."

She smiled. "Thank you."

She sat back with a sense of fullness that had nothing to do with the amount of food she'd eaten. Everyone had finished eating several minutes ago, yet the kids were still at the table, gazing worshipfully at Alex, hanging on his every word.

She had worried earlier that Noah might resent Alex's intrusion into their intimate family circle. It was usually he the kids looked to for teasing and advice. Apparently she had worried for nothing. Noah seemed genuinely pleased to have Alex join them for dinner.

And Alex. She wasn't sure how she felt about the natural way he seemed to fit across the table from her, sharing a meal, sharing the family. He shouldn't fit. He was a bull rider—not at all acceptable.

Still . . .

"Company," Noah said.

An instant later headlights cut a swath across the back porch as a car pulled up in the driveway.

Alex frowned. "That looks like Clint's pickup."

Outside, doors slammed. Inside, chairs scraped across the kitchen floor as everyone rose. Maggie reached the back door first and threw it open to find Clint and Lacey walking up the sidewalk.

Maggie flipped on the porch light. "What a surprise! Come in."

And she *was* surprised. Clint, of course, would have no reason to come out to the house, except with Lacey. And even though Lacey and Maggie had been best friends since grade school, Lacey hadn't been out to the house more than a couple of times since she and Clint had married last summer. There had been no time, Maggie knew, for a new bride who had started back to college and was helping her husband campaign. Maggie was truly pleased to see them.

"We can only stay a minute," Lacey claimed. "We're on our way to Clint's parents', but we just had to stop by and tell you our news."

"Well, you can at least come in to tell it," Maggie said.

"Alex!" Lacey cried. "I'm glad you're here."

Clint followed Lacey inside and stood with his arm around her waist.

As always when she saw how happy Clint had made her best friend since their marriage last summer, a painful lump rose in Maggie's throat. Never had two people deserved happiness as much as Clint and Lacey, and never had two people been so right for each other.

Tonight, whatever their news was, it must be good. Lacey was practically glowing. And Clint—the look in his eyes when he gazed at his wife seemed even more tender, more loving than usual.

"What's up?" Alex asked.

Clint slipped behind Lacey and wrapped both arms around her waist. Lacey leaned back against his chest and placed her arms over his, arching her neck and giving him a soft, secret smile.

Clint grinned. "Well, tell them."

Lacey looked at Maggie, eyes sparkling, face aglow. "We're pregnant, Magoo."

"Oh." Maggie's breath caught. She looked from one to the other, knowing how desperately they both wanted a child. "Oh!" And then she shrieked with delight and launched herself at the couple, reaching to wrap her arms around them both.

Maggie felt their tremendous pleasure, their sheer happiness as if it were her own. For one brief instant, she shared it, remembering the feeling as if it had been only yesterday when she herself had made a similar announcement for the first time.

Then she imagined saying the words again, meaning them for herself, again, now. Another child. Hers.

She felt small and petty, knowing the stinging around her heart was caused by stabs of envy. How selfish. She hugged Lacey tighter. "I'm so pleased, so pleased, Lacey, for both of you, all of you."

Maggie let go and stepped back, one hand going automatically to her abdomen. She already had three beautiful children of her own. She had no business being envious of her best friend. No business wanting another child.

She glanced sideways, and her heart gave a funny little leap.

No business wanting to see a child of hers with bronze skin and black hair and the darkest brown eyes in the world.

Oh, my God.

It was all she could do to keep from running from the room. She swallowed the scream of sheer hysteria threatening to choke her. Happy, excited voices turned into a buzzing in her ears. The room darkened and narrowed until she could see only him, only Alex.

He was shaking Clint's hand and kissing Lacey at the same time. When he stood back, his gaze caught hers.

Maggie squeezed her eyes shut. If he looked in her eyes, he would know. He would see into her heart to things she had only just realized, dreams she hadn't known she dreamed, the wanting, the yearning. *No.* No. He couldn't see those things, please, God. She didn't want to feel them, didn't want to know they were there at all. If he saw them, if he knew they were there in her heart . . . *No.*

Petty, to think of herself when the night plainly belonged to Lacey and Clint. Small, so small of her to feel the envy, to acknowledge it.

She opened her eyes. Alex was still there, looking at her, holding her with his intense gaze.

Through all the congratulations, through answering the childish questions from the kids, through the buzzing in her ears and the darkness around the edges of her vision, the darkness that threatened to overwhelm her, Maggie must have said and done the right things, made the right moves, for no one but Alex seemed to notice anything was wrong.

And it was wrong. As wrong as sin. She couldn't. Dear God, she surely couldn't . . . couldn't have fallen for Alex Dillon. *No, please, no.* Not him. Not a man who, as sure as the world, would climb up on the back of the next Brahma that came charging and snorting and bucking its way through town.

No!

Something had happened tonight. Alex stood just outside Cody's stall in the dark barn, breathing in the familiar, comforting pleasantness of wheat straw, alfalfa, horse, and manure. Something about Lacey and

Clint's announcement about the baby. Alex didn't know what had gone through Maggie's mind, but something sure had.

She had been genuinely happy for Clint and Lacey. She had looked at Alex with the light of joy in her eyes. Then the joy had been replaced by shock, followed rapidly by so many fleeting emotions he hadn't been able to name them.

What had happened? What could she have seen or thought or felt when she looked at him?

He shook his head. "I don't understand, Cody. I don't understand her, I don't understand me."

No, he didn't understand a lot of things. He only knew that in the short time he'd known Maggie, he'd become addicted to the sight of her, the sound of her voice, the taste of her lips. Whatever was happening to him, he had to pursue it. At least until he figured out what the hell it was.

But it seemed, over the next few days, that Maggie had other ideas. It didn't take a genius to realize she was trying to avoid him. The night she'd invited him to supper, she'd smiled and laughed and seemed at ease with him, really at ease, for the first time. Until Clint and Lacey came.

After that, she didn't smile or laugh or even look him in the eye. Wouldn't even speak to him except to answer a direct question.

He wondered how long it would take her to realize she couldn't avoid him, couldn't discourage him. No more than she would be able to keep her kids from climbing trees. In this respect Alex was like a child being told he couldn't do what he wanted most to do. So he would do it anyway, despite her objections. He would get close to Maggie Randolph and learn why he felt he had to.

"Tom," he said to his morning help at the feed store, "I'm headed to the café for lunch."

Tom Two Feathers closed the cash register and gave him a funny look. "You never leave for lunch."

"I do now." Ever since a certain woman started trying to avoid him. Again. It was time, as Noah would say, to rattle her cage.

If Maggie had been the type, she would have stamped her foot in rage. Since she couldn't quite bring herself to do something so stupid, she carried a stack of dirty dishes to the kitchen and whacked them down on the counter. It was bad enough to have to serve Alex his breakfast every morning when she came to work; it was worse yet to run into him every evening at home. He always seemed to be nearby if she so much as stuck her nose out the door, and nearly every night he stopped by the house to talk to Noah about something. Her children only made it worse by using Alex's name in at least every other sentence.

But now! Now he had to show up at the café for lunch.

What would she have to do to get away from him? Leave the country?

The ache inside her grew stronger each day. The ache to talk to him, be with him, get to know him. How was she supposed to stop these feelings that swamped her, these terrible yearnings for his arms, his lips, if every time she turned around he was there?

Just like you do everything else, Magoo. One step at a time.

And that's how she waited on him a few minutes later, too. One step at a time. And she lived through it. Barely.

But that afternoon at home she practically flinched

every time Noah or one of the children said Alex's name. At dinner Stephen was telling her—she was the only one in the family who had missed it—of watching Alex work Cody. It had happened Sunday afternoon, so Maggie had heard the story three times by now.

". . . and every time that calf took a step, Cody was right there with him. Wouldn't let him go back to the others. It was the neatest thing. How does he do that, Grandpa?"

Maggie forced herself to swallow another bite of macaroni and cheese. Now Noah would start talking about instinct and training. Again.

"Well," Noah said, a twinkle in his eye, "part of it's pure instinct. Some horses are just born with cow sense. Part of it's training. That Alex, he knows what he's doin' with that horse."

"He's real smart, isn't he?"

Maggie couldn't help it. The words, "Who, the horse?" just popped out of her mouth.

Four faces turned her way and frowned.

"I *meant* Alex," Stephen said.

"He'd have to be smart," Cindy said. "He said he would build us a tree house, and you have to be sm—"

"He *what?*" Maggie felt the fork bend in her hand.

"Now you've done it," Doug said to Cindy with all the scorn of an older, wiser brother to a little sister.

With rage clouding her vision, Maggie carefully placed her fork across her plate. "Excuse me." She slowly pushed her chair back from the table. With deliberate steps, she crossed to the back door and let herself out onto the porch, making sure the door closed firmly but gently behind her.

With a casualness that belied the steam shooting through her veins, she walked across the hard-packed ground under the glow of the utility light and knocked on Alex's door.

The door opened and light spilled into Maggie's eyes.

"Maggie?"

She took the two aluminum steps and brushed past him into the trailer. "You sound surprised to see me."

"I am." He closed the door. "I gather you think I shouldn't be."

She turned and faced him, her fingernails digging gouges in her palms. She ignored the way the kitchen light struck his high cheekbones and made them gleam. She told herself she didn't care at all that one lock of that silky black hair needed pushing off his forehead. It didn't matter. None of that mattered.

She glared at him. "I don't see how you could possibly be surprised to see me after you told my kids you'd build them a tree house. A *tree* house, for crying out loud!" She flung an arm in the air. "After Doug nearly broke his neck falling out of a tree? How *dare* you say such a thing to them! How *dare* you?"

"Are you finished?"

How could he stand there so calm and cool, when she felt like strangling him? "I've only just started."

"Well, before you serve my head up on a platter, I think you ought to get your facts straight."

"What facts are those?"

"What I actually said to your kids was that I would talk to you about the possibility of a tree house. I made it clear I wasn't making any promises."

"You obviously didn't make it very damn clear. I've just been informed—at my own dinner table, no less—that *you* are going to build a tree house for *my* children. *I'm* here to inform you, in no uncertain terms, that you are not to mention the word *tree* around my children again. There will be no tree house. Not now, not ever, do you hear me?"

"I think you're making a mistake."

"I don't care what you think. If I am making a mistake, it's my mistake. I'll make it if I want, and it's none of your business. None of us are any of your business."

His face went hard around the edges. "Just like it was none of my business a week ago when Doug fell out of the tree?"

She felt the blush but ignored it. "That's not the point."

"That's exactly the point, Maggie, and you're purposely missing it. As usual, you've got your head stuck in the sand when it comes to your protective instincts."

"My head in the sand? What's that supposed to mean? I will not encourage my kids to climb trees and get themselves hurt."

"*That's* my point. You've never encouraged them to climb trees. In fact, you've expressly forbidden it."

"Yes." She nodded emphatically. "Yes, I have."

"And look what happened."

"What—oh, no you don't. You're not going to tell me Doug's accident was my fault."

Alex rolled his gaze toward the ceiling. "Of course not. It was just what you said—an accident. Caused by a young boy's curiosity and eagerness to do what comes naturally to all kids."

She folded her arms across her chest, irritation sizzling through her veins. "Is this leading someplace?"

Alex sighed. "I can tell you're in no mood to listen, but I'm going to say it anyway. Kids are going to do kid things, Maggie, things like climb trees, no matter what their mothers tell them. If they don't think they can get away with it at home, they'll do it at a friend's house."

He walked past her to the tiny refrigerator and pulled out a soft drink. "Want one?"

She glared at him. "No."

He popped the top and leaned a hip against the cabinet. "Anyway," he said, "seems to me you've got two choices here. You can either teach your kids to do those things they're going to do, like climb trees, as safely as possible and lay down a few rules, or you can hold your breath and let them do it the best they can behind your back."

Then he shrugged. "Of course, it's safer for you to do the latter."

"Not according to your philosophy."

"No, according to yours. If you just ignore the reality and keep telling them they're not allowed to do those things, then if an accident does happen, like with Doug, you have a clear conscience. You did the forbidding, Doug broke the rules. You don't have to blame yourself. You kept telling him he'd get hurt, and by golly, look how right you were."

Maggie lowered her arms to her sides. "How dare you talk to me like this?"

"And while we're on the subject, trees aren't the only things those kids of yours aren't afraid of. You should see the way they look at Cody. After the tree house is built, you might want to think about letting me teach them how to ride, before they take it into their heads to learn on their own."

"*You?*" she shrieked. "A *bull* rider? Heaven forbid! You'd be the last person in the world I'd let teach my kids how to ride."

"I'm not going to encourage them to run off and

join the damn rodeo, Maggie. I just want to teach them to ride a horse so they won't try to learn on their own."

"No. Absolutely not. Not now, not ever. You stay away from my kids, Alex, I mean it. Stay away from me, too. We don't need you. We don't want you."

He looked her straight in the eye, not even flinching at her harsh words, words that shamed her with their rudeness. "There's where you're wrong again, Maggie. You do need me. You do want me. And that, I think, more than bulls or horses or trees, is what scares the daylights out of you."

She left then. Shaking from head to toe with fury, she spun on her heel and stormed out the door.

She wasn't the only one shaking. Alex turned and braced himself on the kitchen counter. His arms and legs quivered from the strain of not following her, not dragging her back inside by the hair of her head and making her see the truth.

The hair of her head? He laughed harshly at himself and wondered where these caveman tendencies he'd been exhibiting lately had sprung from.

But he'd been right. The look on her face told him so. She *did* need him, *did* want him. No matter what she said or how she acted, that much he knew. It was all he needed to know.

NINE

Maggie pulled the last towel from the dryer and folded it, then added it to the pile. It was a relief to be home during the day and know that Alex wasn't around. He'd been around everywhere lately, everywhere she'd been. She picked up the stack of clean towels and left the laundry room with a sigh.

Her reprieve from Alex wouldn't last long. The feed store closed at one on Saturdays. That meant he'd be home soon after, and it was nearly eleven now. She didn't have much freedom left for the day.

On her way to the stairs she passed the back door and glanced out. Cindy was "helping" Noah work on the tractor, while Doug and Stephen hung on the corral fence. That was all right, because Maggie had seen Alex turn Cody out in the pasture at sunup, so the horse wasn't in the corral.

So what, then, were the boys staring at so intently? She leaned toward the door. Both boys gazed longingly out at . . . oh, my. They were gazing longingly *beyond* the corral to the horse that grazed in the pasture. Oh, my.

Maggie turned from the door and carried the towels upstairs to the linen closet. Her mouth was dry and her hands shook. It was time for another dose of reality. Time to admit her boys, and maybe even Cindy, were *not* afraid of horses.

Was Alex right? Would horses be the next thing the kids tried without her permission?

She put the last towel away, then went to her room and sat on the bed. She tucked her freezing hands under her arms to warm them. What was she going to do? Give in to something she had fought against for so long and let the kids learn to ride?

If they don't already know how, you mean.

The coldness seeped into her stomach. Several of the boys' friends had horses. Had they already been riding, even knowing they weren't allowed to? Not being allowed to climb trees hadn't stopped them. Was Alex right? Was it time to teach them, before another accident happened?

Would teaching them to ride guarantee there would be no accidents?

Of course not. But . . .

No. She wasn't ready to face that. Maybe, though, just maybe, there were lesser dangers she could face. Maybe.

She would talk to Noah.

Alex pulled up next to his trailer and cut the engine. Odd. The kids were usually all over the place on Saturday afternoons, but no one was around. Noah's pickup was gone. Maybe they'd had to run to town.

All of them, in Noah's pickup? No. Not with Maggie's van sitting right there.

He shrugged and climbed out of his pickup. He planned to spend the afternoon working with Cody. The two of them had an abundance of excess energy to work off. Cody's was from lack of exercise the past few days. Alex's restlessness came from an entirely different source.

He had purposely worked himself into a state of exhaustion at the feed store every day for the past week, hoping to be too tired at night to think of Maggie, to want Maggie.

It hadn't worked. Today he planned to make Cody cut each and every one of Noah's dozen head of cattle. Maybe twice. He went to the pasture gate and put two fingers to his mouth and whistled. In less than a minute Cody came charging up over the rise, mane and tail flying straight out behind him, clumps of sod flinging this way and that from each hoof.

By the time he had Cody saddled, Noah hadn't returned from wherever he'd gone, and no one had come outside. Curious, and just ornery enough to see if Maggie was hiding from him, Alex tied Cody's reins to the corral fence and went to the back door of the house and knocked. No one answered.

He knocked again and hollered. Nothing. He tried the doorknob, and it turned freely in his hand. "Maggie?" he called. He pushed the door open and poked his head inside. "Maggie? You in here?"

No answer. Would they all crowd themselves into the pickup and leave, with the house unlocked? That didn't make sense.

Of course, Maggie could be upstairs taking a nap or something.

The thought stilled him. He had the nearly irresistible urge to find out. With his eyes closed, he could clearly see Maggie, with her long auburn hair streaming across the pillows, her face, *God, her face*, softened and smiling in her sleep.

He jerked his head back and closed the door.

Work. He needed to work. Ride Cody, groom him, clean the stall, paint the barn, build a road—anything. Anything to take his mind off Maggie.

He was crazy, he knew. She might need him, might want him, as he'd told her a few nights ago, but that didn't mean she liked the idea. Didn't mean she liked *him*. He knew as well as she did he wasn't the man for her.

With his jaws clenched, he retrieved Cody's reins and led the horse to the pasture gate. After closing the gate behind him, Alex swung up into the saddle. "Let's do some work, fella. Let's go cut every one of those cattle from the herd one at a time."

Cody snorted and shook his head.

"Okay, so a dozen head isn't a very big herd. It'll do, boy, it'll do."

They started toward the rise and the north pasture, where the cattle had been for the past week. The wind, for a change, was calm, letting the sun warm the air to a balmy sixty-five degrees, according to the radio on his way home. It was one of those late fall days when the sky was so blue he had to squint against the brightness. He was almost to the rise when he thought he heard voices. He drew Cody to a halt.

A ringing, like a hammer on wood, echoed from the woods to the west. Alex reined Cody that direction and soon came across fresh tire tracks. They appeared to come from the gate behind the garage.

Long before he reached the woods he knew where the entire Randolph family had disappeared to. A moment later he found Noah's pickup backed toward a huge old cottonwood surrounded by blackjacks and cedars, with a few redbuds and pecans here and there for variety.

"Look! It's Alex!"

Alex drew Cody up and stared, his mouth open at the sight before him.

"What's the matter, Dillon?" Maggie said with a grin. "Haven't you ever seen a woman up a tree before?"

Maggie Randolph, in jeans and a sweatshirt, her hair in a ponytail, her face without a trace of makeup, and she was up a tree. Alex shook his head and looked again. She was still there. Maggie and Stephen in the cottonwood, straddling a tree limb at least ten feet off the ground!

"Isn't it neat, Alex?" Doug cried. "We're buildin' a tree house."

Alex couldn't take his eyes off Maggie, but he answered as best he could with "So I see."

By God, she'd done it. She had swallowed her fear and done it. Not only had she given in on the tree climbing issue, she was actually sitting up there helping build a tree house, in which she obviously intended her kids to play.

Maggie, Maggie, you're the most . . . incredible woman.

"Unclimb that horse," Noah said gruffly. "You can take this dang board up there and hammer it in place. Bunch of nonsense, if you ask me, hangin' around in a tree like a bunch of monkeys."

Alex swung down off Cody and dropped the reins to the ground, all the while watching Noah fight to keep from letting the smile in his eyes show on his lips. The old man was about to burst with laughter. Alex knew the feeling.

He looked back up at Maggie while Stephen climbed to a higher branch. Maggie watched her son. Alex felt her struggle to keep the anxiety from her face. And she did it. God, he'd never been so proud of anyone in his life as he was of her in that moment, sitting there in that old cottonwood, watching her son climb around, as Noah said, like a monkey, swallowing her fear and her words of caution.

What a woman.

Noah thrust a half-inch-thick square board at Alex. "Roof," the older man said.

Alex kept his eyes on Maggie. "Right." Suddenly he looked down at the four-foot square in his hands, then back up into the tree. *Would you look at that.* The tree house already had a floor, complete with hinged trapdoor, plus four-by-four posts that looked suspiciously like those old square landscape timbers Alex had seen piled against the garage. There was a post at each corner, plus one more in the middle of each of three sides. The side against the tree trunk wouldn't need support for the roof.

He shook his head and looked back at Maggie. "I'll be damned."

"Mr. Alex said a bad word, Mommy."

Maggie gave Alex a fierce frown. "Shame on him."

Alex pushed his hat back with a thumb. "Sorry, ma'am."

She grinned. "Are you just going to stand there, or are you going to haul that roof up here?"

He looked down at the board in his hand just as Noah took it away from him.

"You're too tall to put the roof on before the sides. Here." Noah handed him a board just as long as the first but only two feet wide.

Alex grinned and thrust it back at Noah. "Pass it to me when I get up there."

Alex couldn't remember the last time he'd climbed a tree, but that didn't slow him down on his way up.

His shoulders barely fit through the trapdoor. But once he was up and onto the platform, Maggie joined him. He had to clench his fists to keep from reaching for her.

"Quit sittin' there starin' at each other and get to work," Noah called. "The thermos is empty and I want another cup of coffee."

Alex gave Maggie a wink, then called back, "Well, don't just stand there jawin', send up that board."

Noah passed up the first side. Maggie held it in place, Alex hammered, and Stephen supplied the nails. In no time at all the roof and the sides, which reached less than halfway to the roof but were tall enough to keep someone from falling out, were in place, and the tree house was snug and sturdy.

Maggie and Alex climbed down, but Stephen stayed. Doug was grounded until his wrist healed.

"Mommy?" Cindy said. "How am I gonna get up there?"

Alex watched Maggie's face, wondering if she had selected the tree on purpose. The crotch where the tree house perched was low compared to that of some of the surrounding trees, but there were no low branches. Cindy couldn't climb up. In fact, Alex doubted that even Doug, several inches taller, would be able to make it.

Maggie smoothed Cindy's hair back. "Well, let's see, honey." She looked at Noah, then at Alex.

"Do you want her to be able to get up there?" Alex asked.

He saw her fight a brief inner battle. "Yes," she finally said.

Alex nodded. "Come on, short stuff." He took Cindy's hand. "Let's see what we can do about this."

Noah produced several pieces of two-by-fours just

long enough to nail sideways on the trunk. They stuck out far enough on each side of the tree to serve as both foot and handholds. A ladder. Sort of. The two men took care to keep the "rungs" close enough together so Cindy could reach from one to the next and climb up to the tree house.

Alex showed her how to do it, cautioning her to keep a tight hold. Then he stood her back on the ground and let her do it herself. He kept one eye on her, one on Maggie.

Maggie had her arms wrapped tight around her middle. Alex moved beside her and draped his arm across her shoulders. She was stiff as a board. He had a fair idea of what was going on inside her head just then, and he admired her more than ever for not letting it show on her face.

"Alex," she whispered, her whole body straining toward her daughter.

"Shhh," he said. "I know. But she's fine. She's being careful. She'll be okay, Mag."

By the time Cindy made it up, Maggie was leaning against him. She let out a breath, and he felt her trembling.

"I made it!" Cindy cried. "See, Mommy? I made it!"

"You keep an eye on her, Stephen," Maggie called.

"I will."

Doug took the disappointment of not being able to inspect the new tree house quite well, Alex thought, for a nine-year-old. The boy helped his grandfather gather tools and scraps and load them into the bed of the pickup.

With his arm still around Maggie's shoulders, Alex said, "Let's go for a walk."

He led her through the scrub to the other side of a

big fat cedar a dozen yards away that blocked them from everyone's view. There, with the sun pouring down through the bare branches of the cottonwoods and blackjacks, Alex turned her toward him, wrapped both arms around her, and did what he'd been dying to do since the minute he'd seen her in that tree. He kissed her. Not the way he wanted to, but swiftly.

"I have never . . ." He kissed her again. ". . . been so proud," one more kiss, "of anyone," and again, "in my life."

"I was scared," she whispered.

He kissed her again. "I know."

"I still am," she said.

"I know." This time he pressed his lips to hers and lingered, tasting, savoring, drowning.

She whispered his name.

He pulled her closer, held her tighter, kissed her harder. He took all she offered and gave her everything he had. The sheer force of the emotions spiraling through him left him shaking. Emotions, and heat. Fiery sensations raced through his blood, making him hotter, harder. He pulled her tighter against him and knew by the way she moved her hips that she felt his hardness. Felt it, and welcomed it.

He got harder.

He tore his mouth from hers and gasped for breath, his heart pounding like a thousand hoofbeats. With a hand to her lower back, he pulled her closer still. "Feel what you do to me? Feel it?"

She shuddered.

"It's not just kissing you or holding you that does it either," he confessed as he nibbled her lips. "I started getting this way the minute I saw you up in that tree."

She grinned against his lips. "You have a thing for women in trees?"

He pulled back slightly and gazed at her face, all of it, from her smooth brow to those deep green eyes, across the three freckles on her nose, to her mouth, puffy from the pressure of his lips. "I have a thing for you."

Her chest heaved against his, and her eyes widened. When she opened her mouth to speak, he covered it with his, afraid of what she might say.

He was drowning. In her arms, in her lips and tongue, in the way her body fit so perfectly with his. Her breasts pressing against his chest felt like heaven. Her hands moving along his back, clutching him, made his knees weak. He felt his control slipping. If things went any farther, he'd have her down on the ground with the sound of dead leaves crackling beneath their thrashing bodies.

The mere thought made him groan.

Purposely, with more willpower than he knew he had, he eased his lips from hers and pushed her head to his shoulder. He rested his cheek against her hair and struggled for breath, for sanity.

"We should go back," she said, sounding as breathless as he was.

"I know." He stroked her back but didn't release her.

"They'll come looking for us."

"Probably."

Finally, when he thought he could bear it, he put his hands on her shoulders and stepped back. Her cheeks were flushed, her eyelids drooping. She looked, he thought with deep satisfaction, like a woman who'd just been kissed, and kissed thoroughly.

They started back toward the others, slowly.

"Thanks for helping with the tree house," Maggie said.

"I enjoyed it."

"Where were you headed on Cody?"

The sun fired deep red highlights in her hair. To keep his hands from doing things they shouldn't, Alex hooked his thumbs over his belt. "I was headed out to work him."

"With the cattle?"

"Yeah."

"Will that take long?"

He shrugged. "Not particularly." He squinted up toward the sun. "Only a couple hours of daylight left anyway."

She tugged a dead leaf off a blackjack limb and started shredding it. "Would you like to come to dinner?"

He glanced at her and found her blushing. His pulse speeded up. "Tonight?"

She threw away a piece of leaf. "If you're free. Sort of a thank you for your help today."

"You already thanked me."

"I know, but . . . well, if you're busy . . ."

"I'm not busy." Was she still so uncertain of him? Couldn't she tell by looking at him he would do anything she asked? "I'd like to come."

"Is seven all right?"

"Seven's fine. I'll be there."

This time Maggie vowed she would not make a fuss. No fancy clothes, no dangling earrings, no—well, maybe just a dab of cologne. She showered, washed her hair, and changed into clean jeans and a plain, tailored blouse. Nothing outrageous.

She cut up the chicken and put it on to stew, then turned her attention to the kids and the house. Later, back in the kitchen, she prepared a salad, put it in the refrigerator, then rolled up her sleeves and started on the dumplings.

Her stomach felt like a half-dozen active butterflies had taken up residence. Was she making a mistake inviting Alex deeper into her life? *Was* she inviting him deeper into her life? Or just to dinner?

No. Not just to dinner. There was more to it than that. She felt something for Alex. She didn't want to, didn't think it was wise or safe, but something propelled her on, kept pushing her toward him. The question was, how hard should she resist?

And the other question—if she didn't resist, where was she headed?

She tossed another handful of flour into the bowl and started kneading the dough.

She didn't know where she was headed with Alex. She only knew he made her feel alive. And in his arms, she felt, for the first time in years, like a woman. That was not a feeling she was ready to give up so soon.

Even if Alex Dillon is the wrong man?

She sprinkled flour onto the dough board and turned the soft ball of dough out of the bowl.

Yes, she thought, maybe even if Alex was the wrong man. It wasn't as though she intended to marry him, for heaven's sake. She just wanted to explore these new feelings more completely. See where they led.

After kneading the dough a few more times, she dusted the rolling pin with flour, then rolled the dough out to about an eighth-inch thickness.

Good grief. Am I actually thinking about . . . having an affair?

She paused in the act of sprinkling more flour on the dough. *You can never have too much flour in the dumplin's, Magoo,* her dad had always said. *Make 'em tough, girl.*

What would her dad say if he knew what she was thinking about Alex Dillon? What would Noah say?

Maggie sprinkled more flour, then folded the dough and rolled it out again.

What she did or didn't do with Alex, what she did or didn't feel for him, was no one's business but hers. She wasn't contemplating moving in with him, for heaven's sake.

No, just letting him do all the things his mouth and hands and eyes have been promising—threatening— since the day I met him.

Her knees went weak. She leaned her forearms against the edge of the counter for support. Good grief. What was she thinking? She couldn't have an affair with Alex, no matter how high he stirred the flames in her blood. She simply wasn't the affair type and she knew it.

From somewhere she would have to find the strength to stop whatever it was that happened between them every time they were together.

With new determination, she straightened and finished preparing the dumplings. At precisely six-thirty she added them one at a time to the pot of simmering chicken.

When she dusted the flour from her hands, she mentally dusted Alex Dillon from her life.

Just then he walked in the back door, and her heart skipped more than a beat. His jeans bore a crisp crease, and he wore ostrich boots rather than his scuffed ropers. His tan corduroy jacket, cut western style, emphasized the width of his shoulders. Beneath the jacket, his shirt was so white it glowed against his dark skin. He was . . . he was every woman's dream.

Their gazes met across the room. The heat in his

brown-black eyes nearly scorched her. The butterflies in her stomach took flight again.

Good grief. I'm supposed to turn away from a man like this? Why? Just because she didn't like what he did for a living?

That brought her up short. These days, he managed the feed store for a living. Maybe he was through with bull riding. Maybe he had no plans to return to the rodeo.

And maybe, maybe she was looking for excuses to throw herself at a man too tempting to resist.

Maggie scarcely took her gaze from Alex all evening. He talked to Noah and the kids and they to him as though he'd always been part of the family, had shared their table every night for years. And through it all, his gaze scarcely left her either.

When he said good night, he lingered a moment, his eyes both hot and tender as he looked at her. He settled his hat on his head and gave her a slow smile. "See ya."

Her knees quivered. "Good night."

She closed the door behind him, and not caring who noticed, she went to the window and watched him strut that cocksure cowboy strut of his all the way to his trailer.

When she finally turned back toward the kitchen, she spotted Alex's corduroy jacket draped across the back of the chair he'd occupied at dinner. Her heart gave a thud. She ran her fingers down the lapel, then, before she could change her mind, she grabbed the coat and headed for the den.

She paused at the door. The kids were watching television; Noah was reading the paper. He peered at her over the top of the page.

"I'm . . . Alex left his jacket. I'm going to take it over to him. I won't be long."

Noah dipped his head back out of sight behind the paper. "Take your time. I'll see the kids get to bed by ten-thirty."

Maggie opened her mouth to protest that she had no intention of being gone that long. It was only nine o'clock. But when she tried to speak, no words came out.

She closed her mouth and headed for the back door.

Outside the night was cool and quiet. Even that lone cricket seemed to be gone. Nothing stirred, not a breeze, nothing.

She set her sights on the light in Alex's living room window and walked slowly across the yard. Her mouth was dry and her palms were damp. She was only returning his coat. It was the neighborly thing to do. He might need it in the morning. He might be going out later tonight. It was Saturday, after all. Surely Alex didn't intend to spend Saturday night alone in his tiny trailer.

The thought that he might be going out unnerved her. Was he seeing another woman?

Another woman?

She had thought it as though he were *seeing* her, which he wasn't. They were merely neighbors, acquaintances. Friends? Maybe. Maybe friends.

But if all she wanted from him was friendship, what was she doing knocking on his door at nine o'clock on a Saturday night with the flimsy excuse of returning his jacket? And why, heaven help her, was her heart pounding so hard?

She heard his footsteps moving from the back of the trailer toward the door. Then the door swung open and there he stood, his broad shoulders nearly blocking out the light behind him.

"Maggie?"

She swallowed, or tried to. It didn't work well with a dry throat. "I, uh . . ." She motioned with his jacket. "You left this. I thought you might need it."

With his hot, hungry eyes locked on hers, he took hold of the jacket and tugged. Her fingers seemed locked on the fabric. She couldn't let go.

He pulled with a slow, steady pressure, and kept pulling, the jacket, and her, until she stood before him in his living room, the door shut behind her.

She couldn't seem to let go of the jacket.

A moment later it ceased to matter. Alex let go of it and put his arms around her, pulling her flush against his chest. Without another word between them, he took her mouth with his in a kiss so fierce, so laced with hunger, she couldn't have pulled away if she'd wanted to.

But that, too, didn't matter, for there was nowhere else on earth Maggie would rather have been at that moment than in Alex Dillon's arms.

His hands and lips and tongue, his entire body, sent messages, steamy, unmistakable messages, to her and asked questions. Questions she didn't dare answer out loud. But she answered as best she could with her own hands and lips and tongue, her own body, as it trembled with excitement against his.

With all these things, she told him, *Yes. Yes, Alex, yes.*

TEN

Alex felt the adrenaline rush through him like wildfire through dry brush. *Maggie, Maggie.* But thinking her name was the best he could do. To say it aloud, he would have to take his mouth from hers, and he couldn't. Not for his life.

When she moaned, his knees shook. That had never happened to him with a woman. Not until Maggie. *Ah, Maggie.* He held her so tight he feared he might crack her ribs, but she held on just as tight. The cotton of her blouse was smooth and soft, but it was in his way. He wanted to feel her, *her*, not her blouse. He tugged her shirttail from the back of her jeans and then he was there, touching her back, feeling her sleek, smooth skin, soft as silk.

She shuddered at his touch, then sighed.

The fire in his loins leaped, the ache intensified.

He couldn't get close enough. He thrust one leg between hers and swallowed the moan that came from her mouth. Their unconscious movements abruptly ended with Maggie backed against the end of the kitchen counter. With his mouth still on hers, his tongue dancing and swirling with hers, he cupped her hips and lifted her to the counter, then nestled himself snugly between her legs.

Yes. He belonged there. He pulled her closer, tighter, until the very heat of her pressed against his own heat and hardness. With her arms hugging him close, she wrapped her legs around him and squeezed. A tiny whimpering sound came from her throat and drove him wild.

Still, he wasn't close enough—*she* wasn't close enough. Their bodies were touching everywhere it was possible to touch, but it wasn't enough. Too many clothes.

He passed a hand along her side, up her ribs. Silk. Her skin was like silk. He needed to slow down, to take it easy, before he pushed too hard, too fast. But when his fingers brushed the soft fabric cupping her breast, he couldn't think of slow or easy. He couldn't think at all.

He filled his hand with her firm softness. She arched into his touch. He flicked the hardening nub of her nipple with his thumb. She tore her mouth free of his and arched farther.

With her head thrown back, eyes closed, mouth open and gasping for breath, she was the most arousing sight Alex could ever imagine. And suddenly touching wasn't enough. He had to see her, all of her.

When he slid his hands from beneath her blouse, she cried out and straightened, pulling slightly away, her hot, anxious gaze searching his. When he reached for her top button, the anxiety left her eyes. Her lids lowered partway.

Alex kept his gaze locked with hers while he fumbled and tugged until her blouse hung loose and open. She blinked, finally releasing him from the snare of her eyes. The unbuttoned blouse revealed the front closure of her white bra and an inch-wide strip of pale flesh all the way down to the waist of her jeans. Only an inch. Just enough to rip the breath from his lungs.

But it still wasn't enough, would never be enough.

With thumb and forefinger he released the clasp on her bra. Then, with his eyes on hers, he pushed the layers of clothing aside. Her eyes slid shut. In shyness? He didn't know.

But now he could look at her, and when he did, his breath caught again. "Maggie . . . you're beautiful, so beautiful." Then he was touching her, trailing his fingers over her creamy flesh, down her ribs, and back up to cup the fullness of her breasts. She inhaled sharply, the movement filling his hands even more.

He stroked her nipples with his thumbs.

She cried out, her eyes squeezed tightly shut.

He started to ask if she liked his touch, but it was a stupid question, an unnecessary waste of breath. He could tell by the look of near-pain on her face just how much she liked it. His hands trembled. Never had a woman responded so totally to his touch. Her reaction humbled him, thrilled him, and made the ache in his loins nearly unbearable.

Touching her, seeing her, was heaven. But it wasn't enough. He had to taste her, now, before he starved to death in her arms. He started with her lips, her tongue. Hot, sweet, familiar tastes. Addictive.

He trailed his tongue and lips down her throat. She arched again, offering herself to him. This time it was Alex who shuddered. He whispered, hot, secret words pouring from him, but he had no idea what he said. The only word he recognized was her name, which he repeated over and over, a litany to help him keep what little control he still had, to keep him from bursting into a ball of flames right there in her arms.

Lower. He trailed kisses lower, down past her collarbone to the swell of her breasts. Lower still, until he closed his mouth over a nipple.

She cried out again and clasped his head to her breast as if afraid he might leave.

Leave? How could he ever leave this spot? The hardened nub would never release his tongue, never let him stop tasting, flicking, suckling. So sweet. Sweeter than anything he'd ever known. *Ah, Maggie, Maggie.*

"Alex," she whispered. "Oh, Alex."

His name on her lips, whispered so desperately, made him desperate. He held her closer, suckled harder, swirled his tongue faster and faster.

He had to fight her hands to reach the other nipple. She didn't want him to leave the first one. But the second one was just as hard, just as sweet, just as addictive.

She squeezed him harder with her legs, rocking, rocking her heat against his, saying his name over and over, as he had said hers only moments ago. He felt her trembling against him.

"Too much," she whispered. She jerked her hips from his and backed across the cabinet. "Too much. I can't . . ."

"No." Alex pulled her back to him roughly. "Don't go, don't leave me." He pressed her intimately against his hips and met her frantic gaze, finding her green eyes nearly black with arousal. His heart pounded harder, his breath came faster. "If you want me half as much as I want you, you can't leave me."

Her fingers gripped his shoulders like iron talons. "Want?" Her eyes widened. "Want? I . . . this is way beyond want. This is *need*."

With one hand at her lower back to hold her against him, he used his other hand to pull her head close. "Then come here."

"No. Please." Her cry was harsh. She tried to pull her hips back. "It's . . . too much." Despite her obvious struggle to hold back, she pushed herself against him.

She was beyond ready, and the mere thought nearly made Alex lose what little control he still had.

"It's okay, Mag, it's okay. Let it happen." He flexed his hips. "Just let it happen."

"No," she said with a moan. She shook her head. "No." Her eyes were wide and hot and nearly black. "Not without you."

"It's okay."

"I want you with me. I'm empty, Alex." She took his hand and pressed it against the front of her jeans. "Here. I'm empty here. Fill me, Alex, fill me."

Alex closed his eyes and swallowed, trembled, his fingers splayed across her zipper. "Are you sure, Maggie?" He opened his eyes and asked again, "Are you sure?"

She didn't answer, only looked at him, her eyes wide, her pulse fluttering in the hollow of her throat, her lips trembling.

"I'm still the same man I was when you met me." God, why was he saying these things? "And you're still you."

"I don't care." She tilted her head back and closed her eyes. "I don't care about any of that, not now, not tonight. Don't make me think tonight."

He gripped her shoulders. "Look at me."

Slowly she opened her eyes. She stared at the ceiling a long moment before straightening and looking at him.

Alex swallowed hard. "I . . . I want more than just

tonight, Maggie. I can't . . . give you what I want to give you, can't take what you're offering, and then just watch you walk away."

"What are you saying? What do you want?"

"I . . ." He pulled her close, her breasts to his chest with nothing more than his shirt between them, and buried his face where her neck and shoulder met. "I don't know. I just can't . . . can't stand the thought that tonight might be all there is for us. I'm not asking for promises, and I can't make any myself." *What are you doing, Dillon? Trying to talk her out of the thing you want most in the world?* "Just . . . don't tell me you're going to walk out of my life tomorrow."

"No." She wrapped her arms around him. "I didn't mean it like that," she cried. "We won't know about tomorrow until it gets here, but right now, we've got tonight. Don't we?"

He drew back and saw the wanting in her eyes. "Yes," he whispered. "We have tonight."

For a moment, she relaxed against him. Then she pulled back. With frantic fingers, she attacked the buttons on his shirt. When she had it open, she pressed her palms to his chest.

Alex shuddered at her touch. She pushed the shirt off his shoulders. He let it slide down his arms, then tossed it aside.

With her eyes locked on his, she leaned forward, bold as brass—leaned until her breasts were pressed against his chest. God, it was . . . heaven. The breath left his lungs. He groaned.

Without taking his eyes from hers, he reached for her hips. "Hang on to me." And with her arms around his neck, her legs around his waist, her bare breasts pressed against his naked chest, he lifted her from the counter and carried her to the bedroom.

She gasped.

He would have laughed if he'd been able. Every step he took thrust his hardness fully, completely against the very heat of her.

"Alex, oh, Alex, hurry."

No, he couldn't laugh.

He stopped beside the bed and kissed her. "There's no hurry. We've got all night."

Maggie moved against him, boldly.

He sucked in his breath. His muscles went rigid.

"You may have all night," she whispered. Then she moved against him again. "I think I've got about thirty seconds—before I explode."

A rectangle of light from the kitchen lit the floor beside them. The only other light filtered in through the blinds from the yard light outside the window. But it was enough that he could see she meant it. She was on the verge of exploding.

Using all the restraint he had, he kissed her softly and flexed his hips. "Be my guest."

"No. Please." She clung to his neck and lowered her legs. "Together. Please."

Her legs wouldn't hold her, but Alex did. He swung her up in his arms and, still holding her, jammed one heel into the bootjack in front of his closet and worked off that boot, then the other.

Then, together, they tumbled to the bed in a tangle of arms and legs and frantic hands. Hands tugging, zippers and snaps giving way, clothing disappearing, but not fast enough. Never fast enough.

Then the clothes were gone, and Maggie lay before him, naked and, oh, so beautiful. He whispered her name, and she answered. He could barely hear her over the blood pounding in his ears. Funny. He could have sworn every drop of his blood was pounding elsewhere, much lower. He was now the one ready to explode.

He tasted her lips, her neck, her shoulder, then made his way back to that sweet, sweet spot at the tip of one breast. She gasped and arched beneath him, her back and hips coming off the bed. He trailed his tongue to the other nipple while he stroked her ribs, her belly, with a hand that wasn't quite steady.

The curls at the juncture of her thighs seemed to reach out for his fingers, pulling them down, down, until he felt the fiery heat at her very core, that part of her that burned, just for him. *Maggie, Maggie.*

Someone groaned. Was it him? Her? It didn't matter.

She was hot and wet and ready for him, and she urged him on with the rhythmic movements of her hips. Then she reached for his shoulders. "Alex . . ."

It was all he needed. He moved over her, his weight braced on his elbows, and watched her face as he sank into her. He tried to watch her face, at least, but the feel of her beneath him, around him, seeping into his heart, was too . . . exquisite. Too much. He closed his eyes to hold it in, afraid it wasn't real, that it would disappear.

But when he pulled back, then pushed forward again, her gasp of pleasure told him it was real. She was real, she was here, she was with him.

And then he stopped thinking altogether as the heat and sensations swept him along on an ancient ride more thrilling, more breathtaking than anything he'd ever known in his life. Empty places inside him, places he hadn't even known existed, began to fill to overflowing, aches he had lived with so long he'd forgotten them eased, replaced by Maggie.

She was everywhere around him, within him. She was everything he hadn't even known he wanted, hadn't realized he needed, and now it seemed that if she disappeared there would be nothing left for him, of him.

The heat and the rhythm built, hotter, faster. The flames leaped higher, his breath grew harsher. Then suddenly—*oh, Maggie*—she climaxed around him, through him, and took him right over the edge with her.

Maggie couldn't stop the tears. They streamed from her eyes and into her hair as she lay beneath Alex. His weight, oh, his weight was go good, so right. It was the only thing that kept her from flying to pieces and letting the sobs she fought take control.

Never, never in her life had she known a woman could come apart like she had just done in his arms. The sheer force of her feelings, both physical and emotional, stunned her.

Alex shifted and started to roll off her.

She hugged him close. "No," she whispered. "Don't leave me."

He raised himself slightly on his elbows, his eyes searching hers, reading every secret she'd ever had. "No." He sipped at the tears from one eye, then the other. "I won't leave you."

He didn't seem to need an explanation for her tears. The tenderness in his gaze told her he understood. Still, she wished she could stop crying. "I'm sorry," she said. "I . . . just can't . . . help it."

"Shhh." He sipped again, then kissed her cheek, her nose, her mouth. "It's all right."

"I just never felt so . . . overwhelmed . . . before."

He kissed her lips again and gave her a soft, crooked grin. "Trust me. Neither have I."

Her tears slowed, and Maggie chuckled. "You can't mean it's been six years for you, too."

His entire body went rigid. His head snapped up, eyes wide and stunned. "Six . . . you mean . . . ? Oh, Christ, Maggie. Six *years*?"

Unable to hold his gaze, she focused on his glorious chest. "What can I say? There just hasn't been anyone . . ." With one finger she drew circles on his chest, smaller and smaller until she reached one nipple. She teased it with a fingernail, amazed at the way it changed and hardened, amazed at the way that made her feel. Amazed at the way her touch made Alex draw a sharp breath and press his hips more firmly against her.

She trailed her gaze up his chest, his throat, over those lips she would never get enough of, until she met his eyes. "There hasn't been anyone, until you."

She felt the shudder that rippled down his body and made him quiver. It made her quiver, too. Then he moved his hips against her again, and she gasped. She felt him growing hard inside her, pulsing, filling her again. "You think," she said with a gasp, "I should . . . make up . . . for lost time?"

He lowered his chest to hers, slowly, slowly, one exquisite inch of flesh and muscle at a time, then wrapped his arms around her. "I think," he said between kisses, "we both should."

And they did. But this time their loving started slowly, flowing over them like sun-warmed honey. Alex took her up to that sharp, piercing edge again, then eased her back down before she could fly apart. She cried out in protest.

"Shhh. Easy, Mag, easy."

Easy? She was dying, coming apart at the seams. Easy? "No. Please." She twisted beneath him and wrapped her legs around his hips, pulling him deeper inside her. "I want—"

He gasped, then groaned.

She moved beneath him again.

There was no more easy.

Their loving turned fierce and hot. They strained toward each other, toward the colored lights waiting to burst in Maggie's head. Toward fulfillment of every dream she had ever had, and a few she'd never dared to dream, toward things she never knew existed, powerful, consuming things. Things more elemental than air to breathe.

Then she was there, flying over the edge.

For one fearful second, she was alone in the vast darkness. Then Alex was there with her, his head thrown back, her name on his lips in a cry that pierced her heart. The colored lights, blinding reds and blues and golds, burst in her brain and showered them both in perfect, exquisite release.

Maggie lay wrapped in Alex's arms, so utterly relaxed and limp she couldn't have moved if her life depended on it. The dim light, the warmth of his body added to the intimacy.

They lay in silence a long time before Alex spoke. "There's a question I've been meaning to ask you."

She heard the smile in his voice. She stretched, feeling like a cat in the sun. "Ask away."

With an elbow on the bed, he braced his head on his palm and looked down at her. "Are your eyes really that green, or do you wear contacts?"

She blinked and grinned. "They're all mine."

"You're not nearsighted?"

"No, why?"

His lips quirked. "I was just trying to figure out how you ended up with a nickname like Magoo."

She laughed and rolled to her back, snuggling her shoulder against his chest. "When Larry was little—"

"Larry?"

"My younger brother. I guess you haven't met him."

"I guess not."

"Anyway when he was little, he couldn't say 'Maggie Sue.' It kept coming out 'Magoo' and just sort of stuck."

His eyes crinkled at the corners. "Maggie Sue?"

"Are you laughing at my name?" she demanded with a mock frown.

"Not me!"

"You'd better not be."

"I wouldn't. I swear . . . Margaret?"

She gave him a mock glare. "It's Margaret Suzanne, if you must know. But if you ever call me that, I'll make you sorry."

"You mean," he said with a slow, devilish grin, "you might get . . . physical? Do unspeakable things to my body?"

She pursed her lips to keep from grinning. "You wish, mister."

A look of tenderness softened his face. He ran a calloused palm over her shoulder and down her arms until he reached her fingers. He brought them to his lips and kissed them one by one, sending shivers of heat down her spine.

"I don't have to wish," he said, his gravelly voice sending another shiver chasing after the first one. "You already do unspeakable things to my body."

Only your body? What about your heart, Alex? But she bit down on the words, forcing them to silence.

Their mere presence in her mind brought back all her uncertainties.

But how, she wondered, could she possibly feel uncertain about anything, lying in Alex Dillon's arms, in his bed, with his strength and warmth all around her?

He stretched his arm up along the bed and put his head down beside hers.

His earlier words came back to her. He was still who he was—a bull rider. She was still the woman who hated and feared the life he led.

Maybe right now, in the intimacy of the semi-darkness, in the aftermath of what they had just shared . . . maybe now was the time to talk about it.

She pressed her hand against his chest. Beneath the firm mound of muscle, his heart beat strong and steady. "Alex?"

His lips nuzzled against her temple. "Hmmm?"

Her heart started pounding; her throat dried up. But she had to ask. If she put it off, she'd never find the nerve again. She took a deep breath. "Why do you ride bulls?"

The hand toying with her hair stilled. Alex stiffened. Silence stretched until it seemed deafening.

She swallowed again. "Alex?"

"Are you sure you want to talk about this now?"

She gave a wry half-laugh. "No. I don't even want to think about it. But it's there, and it won't go away. I just want to understand why a man would put himself through the pain of injuries, through that kind of danger." She forced herself to look him in the eye, all the while trying to disguise the pain and pleading in her voice. "I just want to understand. Aren't you ever afraid?"

Something flickered in his eyes, then he looked away with a shrug.

He *was* afraid! "Then why do you *do* it?" she cried. "Why do you put yourself through that?"

He glanced at the ceiling for a long time, then shook his head. "I don't know how to make you understand. Yes, it can be dangerous, and yes, I risk some painful injuries. But I don't . . . a man doesn't think about those things. You go for the thrill. The rush. Nothing else really matters."

"How can it not matter?"

"You're thinking about Steve."

"And you. It scares me, what you do for fun. It's so dangerous."

He studied her a moment. "Tell me this. Why did you have three children?"

"What?"

"You heard me. The world is overpopulated. Most women get sick, uncomfortable, miserable when they're pregnant. Some still die in childbirth. Others go through all that pain of delivery and the baby dies or has something seriously wrong with it. All those things make the risks I take seem pale. But you risked them all, three times."

"You can't possibly compare bull riding with having children. It's not the same thing at all."

"No, it's not. But I don't think the reasons for doing them are all that different. We do them because we want to. Because it gives us something we couldn't find anywhere else. A . . . a rush, a thrill."

"Must be a *big* thrill," she muttered, not at all pleased with his comparison.

"It was."

"Was?" Past tense?

He shrugged. "That's where my comparison falls apart. I doubt a woman ever loses the thrill of bringing a new life into the world."

"But your thrill? You lost it?"

He shrugged again and stroked her cheek.

For a moment, she was elated. If bull riding had lost its appeal, would he stop? Then her heart quaked. Or would he look for something else, something even more dangerous to give him that thrill he seemed to need? She swallowed but made herself ask. "What thrills you now, Alex?"

His look was solemn and deliberate as he gazed into her eyes. "You do."

A hot tingling shot through her and stole her strength. She fell against his chest, blinking back the sudden sting of tears. "Oh, Alex." She planted kisses up to his neck.

He pulled away. "Maggie, look at me."

She did.

"I meant what I said, Mag. Touching you, being with you, hell, even just thinking about you, gives me a rush stronger than anything I've ever known."

His words stunned her, warmed her, filled her to the brim. "Alex—"

"But I'm still me, Maggie. And I'm not . . . I'm not saying I won't ever get on another bull."

"I know." A pain, sharp and bittersweet, ate at her insides. She closed her eyes against it.

"Do you? Look at me. Do you?"

She looked at him. In his eyes she saw uncertainty and longing. She felt her heart crack around the edges. She'd been right that first night in his trailer. He could destroy her. But right then, she couldn't find the strength to care. "Yes. I do know. I . . . I know, Alex. But we have tonight. Just love me. Now."

As she slipped her arms around him, she felt another shudder, this one frightening in its intensity, rip from his head to his toes.

"Maggie," he whispered. "Oh, Maggie."

ELEVEN

When Alex woke up, he was alone. Nothing new there. He always woke up alone, in his trailer, a motel, wherever he happened to sleep. Alone.

What *was* new was that he felt that aloneness. Felt it in his gut, his chest, his empty arms.

Maggie.

He smelled her fragrance on the pillows and sheets. On his skin. Honeysuckle, sunshine . . . and Maggie. And the unmistakable scent of their lovemaking.

He ached with the need—she had been right, it was past want for him, too—the need to hold her, touch her, look into her eyes. Lose himself in her smile, her heat. Fill those empty places deep inside himself he hadn't even known existed, much less that they were empty.

Maggie.

She had slipped away from him in the early morning hours. Even understanding why she had to leave, he hadn't wanted to let her go. He had wanted to fall asleep with her, wake with her. Make love again.

What was she thinking today, right now? Was she sorry?

God, he hoped not. *Don't be sorry, Maggie. I love you.*

Alex sat straight up in bed, stunned. He loved her? Where the hell had that come from?

Yet even as he tried to deny it, he knew it was true. For the first time in his life, Alex was in love. With a woman who hated and feared the thing he did best—rodeoing.

He fell back against the pillow and threw an arm over his face. "Damnation."

No matter how he looked at the situation, he knew he was in love with Maggie. Desperately, deeply, in love, love of the forever kind. And suddenly he wanted to shout it from the nearest rooftop. *Alex Dillon loves Maggie Randolph!* He wanted to paint it in giant letters across the barn, take out an ad in *The New York Times*.

And just as suddenly, he knew he wanted more than that. He wanted it all. Marriage, family, everything. He wanted to help her raise her children, maybe have another one or two along the way. He wanted to watch the kids grow, wanted to be beside Maggie when her hair and his turned gray.

Maggie.

Then reality set in, abruptly and painfully. He knew she felt something for him, something strong, or last night would never have happened. But just because she had made love with him didn't mean she was in love with him.

She had said she knew he couldn't promise not to ride bulls again. Had she meant it?

Maybe she thought she meant it. But Alex knew he couldn't put Maggie through the fear she would experience if he went back to the rodeo. He would lose her for sure. At the very least, he would hurt her, and hurting her was the last thing he wanted to do.

So it seemed logical that if he wanted Maggie, he would have to give up bull riding, for her sake.

Not too many months ago he would have scoffed at the idea that he would ever leave the rodeo. But even before that last injury, he'd felt the excitement waning. Now, he couldn't honestly say he would miss the bulls if he never rode them again. It just didn't seem to be that important any longer.

But if he didn't ride bulls, what would he do?

The question sounded all too familiar. He'd been asking himself that for weeks, with no answer in sight.

Out in the barn, Cody let out an indignant whinny. He didn't like being cooped up at all, much less in daylight, with no other horses around for company.

Alex grinned. "Probably still misses all those mares at McGee-Winder's."

Mares. Winder.

Ought to be raising and training your own stock . . .

Mares. Anadarko. Russ Miller.

. . . he'd pay top dollar, and you could take your time. For you, he'll wait.

Alex could do it. He knew he could. It wasn't as if he'd never thought about it, he'd just never thought about it for *now*. Training horses and raising his own stock had always been something he thought he might do *later*. Maybe *later* was here. Maybe *later* was *now*.

Of course, Miller had probably found another trainer by now, but there were other training jobs out there. His reputation with horses was sound. All he would have to do would be to put the word out. He could be in business in less than a month.

Maybe it was time. Maybe it was past time.

And maybe, he thought with uncertainty, he was

using all this—Maggie, marriage, family, horse breeding and training—maybe he was using them as an excuse. If he never went back to bull riding, he would never have to know if he'd lost his nerve.

"Damnation." He kicked the covers off his legs and got out of bed. Maggie deserved a man with his head on straight, a man who knew his own mind. A man not afraid of the future. A man who *knew* he wasn't afraid.

Alex was not that man. Would never be that man, if he didn't prove to himself once and for all that he wasn't a coward.

Yet the very proving, if he had the guts to do it, would kill whatever tender feelings Maggie might have for him. He believed that clear down to his toes. Maggie would have nothing more to do with him if he went back to the arena, no matter what she'd said last night.

He curled his fingers into his palms and swore. What was a man supposed to do? Please the woman he loved, and at the same time, let himself off the hook, at the cost of his own sense of self-worth? His honor and courage, if he still had any?

Or was he supposed to hurt the woman he loved, and lose her in the process, just to salvage his own pride?

"Damnation."

He needed a long hard ride. He always thought better on the back of a horse than anywhere else.

On the way home from church, Maggie wondered if it had been a sin to mentally relive her hours last night in Alex's arms when she should have been listening to the preacher give his sermon.

It probably had been a sin, she decided. She just hadn't been able to help herself. Last night . . . Alex

. . . Maggie had never known anything like it. She hadn't wanted to leave his arms.

But with three children and a father-in-law only a few yards away, she simply hadn't been able to bring herself to spend the night in Alex's bed, regardless of how much she had wanted to fall asleep beside him and wake up wrapped in his warmth.

She wanted to see him so badly she ached. And it terrified her. Because she knew in her heart she wouldn't be able to hold on to Alex for long. Sooner or later the rodeo would lure him away.

She knew herself well enough to know she couldn't go through that fear, that agony again, of watching someone she loved risk his life, perhaps get hurt, seriously hurt, maybe even killed. She couldn't, wouldn't go through that again.

She wished he had lied last night and promised he would never ride bulls again. She could have fooled herself into believing him for a while. But no, not Alex. He wouldn't lie.

Damn cowboy honor.

He had made her admit, to him and herself, that she knew she wouldn't have him long.

She muttered a prayer, a selfish one, and determined she would love him as long as she could, as long as he stayed.

Love him?

Yes. She loved him. And heaven help her. Because she knew she was going to lose him. She just prayed it wouldn't be soon.

She didn't see Alex all day. His pickup was parked in its usual spot, but Cody and his saddle were nowhere in sight. It was unusual for Alex to be out on Cody all day. Late in the afternoon Maggie began to worry. The day had turned cold and blustery with a sharp north wind.

She looked out the back window and gnawed her lower lip. Had he had an accident? Was he hurt? What should she do?

It was dusk before he finally rode in from the pasture.

Maggie ran to the hall closet and grabbed her coat. "I'm going to lock up the chickens."

"I thought it was my turn," Doug called from the den.

"I'll do it tonight," she answered on her way out the back door.

By the time she was outside, Alex had made it to the barn, where she couldn't see him. He would have to unsaddle Cody, then cool him down and groom him. She had time.

Most of the chickens had already gone to roost for the night. The rest of them came running and clucking at the sound of grain hitting the feeder.

After filling the feeder, Maggie put out fresh water, gathered the eggs in her wire basket, then shut the door against predators.

Then, as if out for a leisurely walk, she strolled into the barn with her basket of eggs. Alex was walking Cody straight toward her. Maggie could see the steam rising from the chestnut coat.

When Alex saw her, he stopped abruptly. What was he thinking? With his hat pulled low, she couldn't see his eyes, and the turned-up collar of his denim jacket hid his jaw, but his mouth was clenched as tight as his gloved fists. Did he regret last night? Why had he stayed away all day?

Maggie tucked her free hand into her coat pocket. "You were gone a long time."

He shrugged.

"I was . . . worried about you."

A muscle in his jaw flexed.

Maggie's throat tightened. Coming to the barn had been a mistake. Alex obviously didn't want her around. "I can see you're busy. I'm sorry I bothered you." With eyes stinging, she turned to go.

She made it to within three feet of the barn door before he called her name. The gravel in his voice sounded laced with pain. Maggie halted, every muscle tense.

"Maggie, I . . . will you come out to the trailer tonight?"

At the hesitancy in his voice, her tears overflowed. He sounded as though he didn't know if he wanted her to say yes or no. She couldn't bear for him to see her crying, so she kept her back to him and asked, "Do you want me to?"

For a long moment the only sound was Cody blowing.

Oh, God, he doesn't want me to come.

Was it over then between them? So soon? Had she lost him already, and not even to the rodeo? The ache in her chest made her knees quiver. He didn't want—

"*Yes!*"

Maggie flinched. His voice came raw and fierce, as though torn from deep in his gut.

"Will you?" he asked.

She should tell him no. She should run to the house and count her lucky stars things had ended between them so cleanly. He obviously hadn't wanted to say yes, so why had he?

"Will you, Mag?"

Mag.

She closed her eyes. "Yes." Without waiting, she fled the barn.

* * *

The kids were asleep by ten, but Noah didn't turn in for another half hour. Maggie waited in the den, claiming she wasn't sleepy, and listened for the floor above her head to stop creaking, telling her Noah had settled down for the night.

She waited another ten minutes, then slipped on her coat and went to the little trailer next to the barn. She was probably a fool for going. Alex was probably going to tell her something like, "Look, Mag, last night was fun, but we're just too different, you and me." Then he would probably smile and finish her off with, "Let's just shake hands and be friends."

It was coming. She knew it was coming. But she could no more stay away from him after last night than she could stop the wind.

His door opened before she knocked. With the light behind him, she couldn't see his face. He said nothing, merely stepped back and motioned her inside. She took the two aluminum steps and squeezed past him while he shut the door behind her.

She stopped beside the coffee table and stared blindly at one corner of it, not having the vaguest idea what to do or say. She wanted to turn and throw herself at him, wanted to feel his arms hold and shelter her, wanted to feel his heart pounding in time with hers.

"Maggie," he said, the gravel in his voice sounding rougher than usual. "I . . . don't want you to think . . ."

She turned slowly to face him and gasped. The stark yearning in his eyes interrupted her heartbeat. "Alex."

In one stride he was pulling her into his arms and trailing kisses across her face. "Damn it, Maggie, I don't want you to think this is all I want from you, but I can't help it."

Maggie's knees nearly buckled with relief. He wasn't ending anything! He was . . . he was . . . ah, what he was doing with his lips below her ear . . .

"I stayed away all day on purpose. I thought I could make it back inside without seeing you."

She tore off her coat and wound her arms around his neck. "You didn't want to see me?"

His lips and tongue left a trail of fire along her jaw. "I was afraid to see you, afraid I wouldn't be able to keep my hands off you. It was all I could do to keep from grabbing you earlier in the barn."

Maggie's blood rushed and her heart sang with relief as her doubts faded. She dug her fingers through his thick black hair. He wanted her! He still wanted her! "When you wouldn't talk to me I got so scared. I thought . . . I thought you didn't want . . ."

"I want, Maggie." He nipped at her lips. His eyes were dark and haunted. "I think maybe I want too much."

She silenced him with her lips and tongue. The groan she drew from deep inside him shot fire all through her.

He swung her up in his arms and carried her to the bedroom, where he stood her beside the bed. "I wanted to go slow, to make it last." He kissed her again as he unsnapped her jeans. "But I don't think I can."

She tugged open the snaps on his shirt and placed a kiss in the center of his chest. "No," she whispered. "Don't go slow. I can't wait that long."

With another groan he started tugging off her clothes, and Maggie did the same for him. By the time they were undressed and on the bed her breath came in sharp gasps and heat pooled between her legs.

"Alex . . ."

There was nothing slow or easy about the way they loved. Maggie was too aware of fearing she had already lost him, of knowing she would lose him soon. She wouldn't have let him go slow if he'd tried. She was too desperate for his touch, the taste of his skin, the feel of him filling that empty place deep inside her.

And fill her he did, to her very core. He filled her, thrilled her, and took her straight over the edge.

Afterward, Alex got his wish and loved her slow and easy. So slow and easy Maggie blushed to think of how she begged him to hurry. But eons later, when he finally took them over the peak again, she was glad, so glad he hadn't listened to her.

It was a night, along with the one before, that she would remember for the rest of her life.

The next morning when Maggie stumbled to work with a sleepy, satisfied smile, she knew exactly what the phrase "on top of the world" meant. She wasn't certain if her feet were even touching the ground.

The feeling didn't last long. A premonition, dark and foreboding, crept up on her, stealing her happiness. When Alex failed to show up for breakfast at the café, she lied and told herself he'd merely overslept. But deep in her heart she knew better.

Alex really thought he would be able to face Maggie in the daylight after a second night in her arms. He'd been a fool. In the daylight she would see right through him, see there was nothing there but his own uncertainties.

Instead of turning up Main to the café for breakfast, Alex had driven straight to the feed store. Before he saw Maggie again he had to have some answers to the questions that plagued him. He had to know what kind of man he was. Was he good enough for her? Strong enough? How did a man know?

The first thing he had seen when he opened the store had left more questions than answers. His eyes had been drawn immediately to the poster someone had tacked to the bulletin board week before last. The poster Alex had purposely ignored.

He tucked the twenty into the cash drawer and counted out three dollars and fourteen cents change. "There you go, Sam. Thanks." It took considerable concentration to keep from slamming the drawer shut.

All morning he'd felt that damn poster calling to him, mocking him. "Read me, Dillon, come on. You're a big, tough cowboy, surely you can read a simple sign."

Alex purposely kept his gaze away. He didn't need to read the sign; it fairly shouted at him about the local rodeo next week. It shouted, "Here's your chance, Dillon. Can you do it? Can you really climb up onto the back of a Brahma again, or are you yellow?"

It seemed a sacrilege to even think about a rodeo when Maggie's sighs still haunted his mind.

He turned his back on the sign and poured himself a cup of coffee. God, he hated Styrofoam cups. He should bring a mug from the trailer.

He took a sip, then set the cup down and stepped from behind the counter. Had to get that front shelf cleared off to make room for new merchandise.

The front shelf, right next to the bulletin board with that damned rodeo flyer taunting him. He ignored the flyer.

Out on the loading dock loud voices called, too many to distinguish. Then the front door creaked open and Noah Randolph came in.

Alex stiffened. Did Noah know where Maggie had spent the better part of the last two nights?

"Morning'," the old man said easily. No censure, no telling look.

Alex relaxed.

"Got tired of drinkin' my own coffee. Thought I'd come down and drink some of yours."

"Help yourself."

With a nod, Noah stepped behind the counter to the coffeepot. Alex turned back to his shelf.

The voices on the front dock grew louder, then the front door groaned in protest at being slammed open. Five boisterous men sauntered in. Five men Alex had no earthly desire to see.

"Howdy, Dillon," the tallest one said.

Alex nodded. He didn't remember the man's name or the names of the others, but he knew who they were. Rodeo riders, all of them. Deep Fork's best and rowdiest, men who rode anything that bucked. He'd ridden with and against them several times in past years, even though all of them were a good eight or ten years younger than he.

"Just the man we wanted to see," said another.

Alex straightened a display of dog vitamins. "What can I do for you?"

The tallest one pushed his hat back with a thumb. "You can tell us how come the best damned bull rider this county's ever seen ain't signed up for the rodeo next weekend."

He'd known it was coming. Sooner or later someone was bound to ask. Still, Alex wasn't prepared for the icy shiver that raced down his spine.

The shortest of the group—Alex thought his name was Hank—pushed his way forward. "I'm on the sign-up committee. Figured maybe it was just an oversight, your name not being on the list, so we came to check. You wouldn't want one of us to win too easy, now, would you?"

"Don't badger the man, Hank. Hell, he's gettin' old.

Maybe he don't wanna go up against the bunch of us. We're still in our prime."

Alex shrugged. He was used to jokes about his age. They didn't bother him.

" 'Course," the tall one said, "after that last tumble you took up in Wichita, I could see how you might not wanna ride again."

Alex stiffened. From the corner of his eye he saw Noah standing behind the counter taking in the entire scene.

Damnation. What the hell was he supposed to do? This would be the perfect chance to prove to himself he could still ride. But if he was wrong, if he climbed up on that chute and couldn't do it, couldn't lower himself onto the back of a bull, he'd be making a fool of himself, proving himself a coward in front of people he'd known all his life.

He couldn't do it. He couldn't take the chance. Better to find some other rodeo far away. Montana, maybe. If he humiliated himself in some little local Montana rodeo, who the hell would know?

I would.

"Whatsa matter, Dillon?" Hank said with a laugh. "I didn't know better, I'd swear by the look on your face you'd turned chicken."

Alex carefully kept his expression blank as he scanned the faces around the room. He read laughter, good-natured teasing, a hint of respect, and from Noah Randolph, sharp speculation.

Hellfire. He was damned if he did, damned if he didn't. A sick feeling rolled through his stomach. *You're not going to believe this, Maggie, but this is for you.*

He clenched his fists so no one would notice the way his hands shook. "Sign me up."

Hank grinned. "Bull riding?"

Alex clenched his jaw and nodded. "Bull riding."

The conversation turned to a loud buzzing in his ears. He turned back and stared at the shelf on the wall.

"Dillon?"

At the sound of his name, he jerked. He was stunned to find the room empty but for himself and Noah. He swallowed a lump in his throat that tasted suspiciously like fear.

"Do you know what you're doin'?" Noah asked, his blue eyes piercing into Alex's soul

Yeah, he knew what he was doing. He was setting out to prove to himself he was man enough for Maggie. And the very proving of it would end everything they'd ever shared.

He gave a harsh laugh. "Yeah, I know what I'm doing."

Noah took a slow sip of coffee, then set the cup down. "You don't look all that excited about it. I assume you know what this is going to do to Maggie, and from the look of you, it's rippin' at your gut. I gotta ask myself, 'Noah, what the hell's goin' on here? I thought the boy kinda took a shine to Maggie. I know she sure took a shine to him'."

Alex turned sharply away and stared out the window of the front door at the traffic creeping down Main Street. "Let it go, Noah."

"Not on your life, boy."

There it was, the steel in Noah's voice that Alex had known existed but had never heard.

"You tell me," Noah said harshly. "You tell me why you're gonna break that girl's heart by doin' something you know's gonna scare the pants off her. Something it looks to me like you don't even want to do. You tell me why, boy. What are you tryin' to prove?"

The fear inside Alex rose up and threatened to choke him. Fear of losing Maggie. Fear of not being able to ride. He spun on Noah. "I'm trying to prove I can still do it."

Noah blinked. "Still do what, ride bulls?"

"Yes, damn you, *yes*."

Noah turned his head slightly and narrowed his eyes. "Just who," he said slowly, "are you trying to prove it to?"

"Myself!"

Maggie heard about it before the lunch crowd started pouring in at the café. Her hands turned to ice and her stomach heaved. Alex had signed up for the local rodeo next weekend.

She had known she wouldn't have him long, but two days? Was that all she got? Two days, two nights of his precious time before the rodeo lured him away?

Oh, God, she couldn't stand it. The pain nearly crippled her.

Somehow, she managed to make it through the lunch rush, but as soon as the customers trickled down to a few, she did something she hadn't done more than half a dozen times in her life—she left work early. Left work and drove home in a daze.

At home, she wouldn't allow herself to go to her room. If she did that, she knew she would throw herself on the bed and cry herself sick. She felt sick enough already.

So she wandered around the house, not paying attention to anything. She'd been home about thirty minutes when Noah came in from the pasture and asked what she was doing home so early.

She swallowed around the lump in her throat and

tried to get the words out. They wouldn't come. She just shook her head while her eyes filled with tears.

Noah took his bill cap off and whacked it against his leg. "It's about Alex, isn't it?"

She swallowed again. "You've heard about the rodeo?"

He sighed and looked at her with pity. "Yeah, Maggie girl, I heard."

"I've lost him, Noah." She hugged her arms around herself and turned away from him. "I've lost him." Her words, she knew, told Noah more than she had intended to tell him.

His warm hand settled on her shoulder.

But Maggie couldn't take his sympathy or pity just then. She was already feeling sorry enough for herself. "I'm going for a walk." And she fled out the back door toward the woods.

TWELVE

It seemed to Alex as if all of Lincoln County was conspiring to keep him at the feed store so he couldn't give Maggie the courtesy of hearing from his own lips that he'd signed up for the rodeo next weekend. He'd never seen so much business at Sutherland's. He didn't get a chance to leave until after two o'clock.

With a sick feeling growing in his stomach, he rushed up the hill to the café. What was he going to say to her? How would he be able to tell her the one thing he knew she didn't want to hear?

But she wasn't there. According to Barbara, the other waitress, Maggie had gone home nearly an hour earlier.

"Was something wrong?" Alex asked.

Barbara shrugged. "Said she didn't feel well. If you ask me, she didn't look too good either."

Sick? Was Maggie sick?

Alex rushed back to the feed store and got in his pickup. He drove all the way home like the proverbial bat out of hell. Noah was standing on the back porch, the ever-present cup of coffee in his hand.

"Where is she?" Alex demanded. "They said at the café she came home sick. Is she all right? What's wrong?"

Noah pursed his lips, narrowed his eyes, and took a sip from his mug. "She's not sick. Not like you mean, anyhow."

Alex felt a lurching in his stomach. "She heard."

"In a town this size? Hell yes, she heard."

Alex closed his eyes and turned his face into the sharp wind. "Where is she?" He straightened his neck and glared at Noah, silently urging, commanding the man to answer.

"Well now." Noah took another sip. "Don't know as I ought to be tellin' you that."

"Damn it, old man, you tell me where she is. I have to talk to her."

Noah stared at him a moment—a long moment—then nodded slowly. "She took off toward the west pond."

"Noah, I—"

But Noah didn't stay to hear what Alex had to say. The older man turned his back and went inside. Just as well. Alex didn't have the vaguest idea what to say to him.

He realized on his way to the pond that he didn't know what to say to Maggie either. What was there to say? He'd signed up for the bull riding.

Maggie, trust me. Please. Could he ask her that? What would he tell her? That it was all right, because no matter what happened this weekend, it would in all likelihood be his last bull ride?

No point in telling her that. She wouldn't believe him.

Besides, if he climbed into that chute and found he didn't have the nerve to ride the bull, he'd never be able to face Maggie again, so what was the point in asking her to wait, to trust him? There was no point.

The whole thing was stupid. A man ought to be able to look inside his own mind, his own heart and *know* what he was and was not afraid of. And to a certain extent, Alex could do that.

But only to a certain extent. When he tried to picture himself climbing onto the back of the bull, the gate opening, the bull charging out bucking and twisting, he couldn't. All he could seem to see was a gray, cloudy sky overhead while he lay on his back in the arena dirt. Then the shadow, dark and angry and snorting, moving over him. And hooves. Coming straight for his head.

That very thing had happened to him more than once. He'd always been able to roll away in time. Or in enough time to live to tell about it. But when he pictured it now, he pictured himself freezing in total terror, unable to move.

That had never happened to him, that terror. Not in the arena.

But would it this time?

That's what I have to find out. Will I even be able to get on a bull? And if I can, and if I end up in the dirt, will I be able to scramble away like I've always done, or will I freeze?

It was stupid. A man should know himself well enough to answer questions like those. A man should know what he feared.

He knew the one thing he feared more than anything was losing Maggie. But a close second was the fear of losing his own self-respect, his sense of self-worth. How could he ask Maggie to share her life with a man who couldn't face himself?

He couldn't ask her. It was that simple. Maggie deserved better.

Hell, he thought, stretching his legs out farther, eating up the distance between him and Maggie as fast as he could. No matter how Saturday turned out, Maggie deserved better than him. She deserved a man who wouldn't hurt her the way he had today. A man with the sense and strength to stay away and keep his hands to himself until he knew who and what he was.

But no, Alex hadn't been able to do that for her. He hadn't been strong enough. Her pull had been too great to resist.

He found her sitting on the grass dam that kept the creek from flowing westward out of the woods at the edge of the pasture. She had to have seen and heard him by now, but she didn't look up. He kept his gaze on her as he rounded the pond.

She sat cross-legged on the ground, breaking little pieces off a long twig and throwing them one by one into the pond. The wind played with her unbound hair, tossing it around her head and across her face. She made no move to push the curls aside, just kept staring at the twig in her hands and tossing bits of it into the pond.

Alex jumped across the runoff stream and in three strides was on the dam. Maggie was less than ten yards away, but she still hadn't looked at him.

He stuffed his hands into his back pockets, suddenly noticing how cold the wind was, wishing he'd thought to wear a jacket.

Maggie hadn't worn a jacket either, and as Alex drew closer, he could see her shivering. No telling how long she'd been sitting out here on the cold ground with the north wind cutting through her. He wanted to huddle down beside her and shelter her from the wind and cold. Wanted to wrap his arms around her and bury his face in that wild, red hair. Wanted to weep against her neck like a baby and beg her not to give up on him.

But he couldn't do any of those things. He stopped beside her and waited. Still, she didn't acknowledge him.

"Maggie?"

No answer.

He sank to his knees beside her. "Maggie, look at me."

Her fingers stopped playing with the twig. The wind whipped her hair aside, and Alex saw her face clearly in profile. She was staring at the stick as though she had no idea what it was or how it came to be in her hand. Then she tossed the stick out into the water and stared after it.

She wrapped her arms around her middle and gave a harsh laugh. The sound of it cut through Alex like an ax.

Maggie shook her head, still staring at the pond. "You said you wanted more than just one night." She laughed again. "Silly me, I thought you meant at least a week. I didn't know that by more than one night, you meant two."

Alex clenched his jaws against the pain. He clenched his fists against reaching out to touch her. Every muscle in her body fairly shouted at him to keep away.

"Guess I know where that leaves me on the list of important things in Alex Dillon's life."

Maggie, I'm sorry. "You have no idea how important you are to me."

"Don't I?"

She looked at him then, and he wished she hadn't. The calm, empty look in her eyes nearly killed him.

She faced the pond again. "It's funny, you know? I thought we had something pretty special going for us.

I really thought you . . . well, it doesn't matter what I thought, does it?"

"It does matter." His words felt raw in his throat. He grasped her upper arm and turned her toward him. "We *do* have something special, Maggie, more special than anything I've ever known, and it doesn't have to be over."

Her eyes widened. "Doesn't have to be over?" she cried. "Of course it's over. You can't seriously expect me to kiss you on the cheek and send you off on your merry way to break your damn neck. I've lived through that once. Literally. I won't do it again. I can't, Alex. I thought you knew that."

Alex closed his eyes briefly. If he told her the reason he'd signed up for Saturday, would it make any difference? Would she understand? Would she wait for him?

But then, what if he found he couldn't ride? She would be waiting for a man who would never be able to face her again.

No. He couldn't tell her.

With a sick feeling in his gut, he opened his eyes and looked at her. "I do know that. I'm not asking you to put yourself through that again. I don't expect you to come watch me ride. I don't *want* you there. There are things you don't understand—"

"Now there's an understatement."

"—things I can't explain."

"There's nothing to explain."

"Can you trust me, Maggie, for just a little longer?"

"Trust you?" She let out another harsh laugh. "Trust you? I *love* you. Look where that's gotten me. Absolutely nowhere. What good is trusting now?"

It was all Alex could do to keep from doubling over with pain, or pulling her into his arms. She loved him.

God, Maggie.

"Go away, Alex." She turned her face away, but just before she did, he saw that blank look come across her eyes again. "Just go away. You, your horse, your trailer. Please. I'm asking you this time. Please go away."

That night, for the first time in years and years, Maggie buried her face in her pillow and cried herself to sleep. The rodeo had ripped another man from her life.

But the next morning she found out that this second time was different from the first. Maybe even worse. Because Alex wasn't gone, wasn't dead. He had the absolute gall, after tearing her life, her heart to pieces, to show up at the café for breakfast.

At least he didn't sit in her section, thank God. His very presence made her hands shake and her throat shut tight on tears she didn't know she had left. If she'd had to wait on him . . . no, God couldn't be that cruel.

Then Alex came back for lunch.

And apparently he started leaving the feed store early, because he was back at the ranch well before sundown every day the rest of the week. She knew, because every time she looked out the window, he was there.

He seemed to be everywhere, and it was killing her. How was she supposed to heal if he was always around?

"Damn him, why doesn't he just go away?"

"I assume you're talking about Alex."

Startled, Maggie whirled to face Noah standing in the doorway from the kitchen to the dining room. She hadn't known he was there, much less that she had spoken her words aloud.

The shrewd look in his narrowed eyes set her back up. Anger felt better than the tears she constantly battled these days. "Of course I'm talking about Alex. I can't think of anyone else I'd love to see disappear from my life."

Noah pulled a toothpick from his shirt pocket and flicked the end of it with a forefinger. "What makes me think you don't really mean that?"

Naturally Noah would see through her anger. But couldn't he see through it far enough to find the fear and the pain? "I do mean it, Noah."

"From what I've seen around here lately, I would have said you were in love with him."

He saw too much. She sighed. "And look where it got me. The first chance he gets, he goes out and signs up for the nearest rodeo. I can't live with that, Noah. You, of all people, should understand that. He understands it, too. I guess he just doesn't care enough."

Noah tucked the toothpick between his teeth. "Oh, I don't know. It's not like he signed up to ride Saturday just to make you mad, or just to hurt you. The man's got his reasons, Maggie."

"I'm sure he does." She remembered what Alex had told her about the thrill he got on the back of a bull. That seemed to be reason enough for any rodeo cowboy. "But I can't live with it. You know that."

Noah smiled sadly. "Yeah, Maggie girl, I know."

Alex stepped up onto the sidewalk in front of the café and paused before reaching for the door. Why did he keep putting himself through this torture of seeing Maggie every chance he got, only to have her stare past him with dull, empty eyes?

He had put that look in her eyes. He and his damned fear, his inability to stay away from her when he'd known all along he should have. The kindest thing he could do for her right now would be to stay away from her, at least until after the rodeo tomorrow.

Yet here he stood, his hand reaching for the doorknob that would take him into the café.

How the hell was he supposed to stay away from her after she told him she loved him? God, it had been all he could do not to tell her how much he loved her, how much he was afraid of losing her forever. How he was afraid of losing himself, too, and that *that* was why he had to ride Saturday. If he lost himself, there would be nothing left to give to Maggie.

And he wanted to give to Maggie. He wanted to give her everything. Himself, his love, his life, his very soul.

He hoped, if tomorrow went all right, if he hadn't lost his nerve, that things would work out. He already knew tomorrow would be his last ride. He prayed Maggie would take him back.

But every day that possibility looked less and less likely.

Still, he couldn't bring himself to stay away from her.

He grabbed the brass knob, turned it, and pushed the door open. The smell of fried onions hit him in the face. George Jones wailed from the jukebox. That's all Alex needed—George Jones singing "He Stopped Loving Her Today." A song about a dead man. Terrific. It nearly drowned out the tinkle of the bell above the door announcing his entrance.

He pushed the door shut and searched for an empty seat. Lunch was unusually busy today. There was only one empty booth. It was on Maggie's side. He took it anyway.

He watched the swinging door to the kitchen, his chest aching for the sight of Maggie. When she came through a moment later carrying three burger baskets, her gaze caught his and, for an instant, she froze.

God, the pain in her eyes. *Maggie.*

All he wanted to do was love her, but somehow it had all gone wrong.

He watched her straighten her shoulders and square her jaw. The look of firm resolve that came over her face tore at him. He could almost read her thoughts. She wanted nothing more to do with him, and she was getting sick and tired of his showing up every time she turned around.

He should have stayed away. He just hadn't been able to.

She didn't look at him again, not even a glance from the corner of her eye. He knew, because he didn't take his gaze off her for a minute. Even when she brought him water and stood next to his table with her pad and pencil ready, she still didn't look at him.

He was almost glad. Anything was better than that blank, lifeless look he'd seen that day at the pond.

But he couldn't stand her not looking at him. "I noticed your van parked outside."

She didn't answer, didn't look at him.

He couldn't blame her. He sounded stupid. "Your right rear tire is low."

Still no response.

"You should have it checked."

She stood beside him and stared at her order pad. "Do you want lunch, or what?"

He reached for her hand. "Maggie, I—"

She snatched her hand from his. "Don't."

Her withdrawal stung. He should have expected it, knew he deserved it, yet her reaction angered him. He gave her a sarcastic smile. "Sorry. For a minute there I had you mixed up with somebody else. Her name was

Maggie, too." *Shut up, Dillon. This isn't fair.* But he couldn't stop. "Wasn't all that long ago she seemed to like me touching her. She even said she loved me."

As he watched the blood drain from her face, he called himself every vile name he could think of. "Maggie, I'm sorry."

Then, before his eyes, her face changed, turned hard. "No, you were right. That must have been some other woman. Funny how some women are so stupid as to fall for a fool with a death wish. Just how does a man talk himself into crawling up on an animal whose prime purpose in life is to throw him to the ground and stomp him into little pieces? Where do you get your nerve?"

Alex jerked his gaze from hers. *Don't let her see. Don't let her look in your eyes.* For something to do with his hands other than pound his fist through the table, he reached for his glass of water, not at all surprised to notice his hand wasn't quite steady. *Where do you get your nerve?* "Let's just hope I didn't inherit it from my old man."

For the rest of the day Maggie tried to keep her mind blank. It was impossible. The picture of Alex's face, that sharp flash in his eyes of what she swore had to have been fear would not go away. What had he been thinking just then?

And why had she said those awful words? Why?

But she knew why. She was hurt and angry and had wanted to lash out at him. So she had lashed.

She had lashed, and he had sipped water. Then he had picked up his hat from the seat beside him, settled it on his head, and slid out of the booth. Without a word, without even looking at her again, he had sauntered out of the café with that lazy, lean-hipped gait that made her think of the way he had rolled his hips against hers while he was buried deep inside her, taking her breath away. Just thinking of it still took her breath away.

Damn you, Alex Dillon. How was she supposed to live through tomorrow? For that matter, how was she supposed to live through today, tonight, after the ugly things she had said to him?

And what had he meant about inheriting his nerve from his father?

She dreaded seeing him again at home that afternoon. Would she hide from him the way she'd been doing all week?

Of course I will.

But he didn't come home early that afternoon as he had the past several days. Maggie knew, because she kept looking out the back window toward his trailer every few minutes, watching for his pickup. It never came.

After dinner the kids scampered to the den to watch one of the movies Noah had rented for them that afternoon. He'd rented six. When she questioned him, he had said he just felt like giving the kids a treat for the weekend.

As preoccupied as she was, she was grateful the kids had something to do. She felt guilty for paying so little attention to them, particularly this afternoon. But she couldn't concentrate for thinking of Alex, of that look on his face, the remark about his father.

She rinsed a plate and stacked it in the dishwasher, then reached for the next one. Had that really been fear in his eyes today?

Suddenly she remembered that night on the back porch, the night after Doug had fallen from the tree. Alex had talked about fear, about how it made a person clumsy and broke his concentration.

Then she remembered Monday, when he'd found her at the pond. *I don't expect you to come watch me ride. I don't want you there. There are things you don't understand . . . things I can't explain.*

With the memory of those words, and the look on his face today in the café, Maggie knew with certainty, clear down to her soul, that there was more going on here than just another bull ride. A chill swept through her. Something was wrong. Something terrible was happening, and it had to do with Alex. But she'd been so wrapped up in her own misery she hadn't been paying attention.

With a sharp twist, she turned off the water and grabbed a dish towel. On the way to the den she dried her hands and took a deep breath to help slow her racing pulse.

"Noah, can you come in here a minute?"

Noah followed her back to the kitchen, where she whirled to face him. "What do you know about Alex's father?"

Noah looked surprised. "Lee?" He shrugged. "What do you want to know?"

Maggie twisted the dish towel into a knot. "I don't know. Alex said something today, and I just wondered."

A strange look came over Noah's face. He turned his head sideways and looked at her out of one eye. "What did Alex say?"

Maggie hung her head. "Oh, Noah, I . . . I said terrible things to him. I—" A sob clogged her throat and cut off her words. A moment later she felt Noah's hand on her shoulder.

"Tell me, Maggie girl," he said softly. "Tell me what happened."

Maggie choked back her tears and wiped her eyes,

but she couldn't look Noah in the face. She was too ashamed of her own behavior during the past week. Yet she managed, haltingly, to tell him what had happened that afternoon in the café.

"Good God, girl, what the hell'd you go and say a thing like that for? Don't you know better than to make a man who's about to do something dangerous think about fear?"

Maggie felt the old familiar question rise to her lips—the question she'd never dared to ask. This time, it asked itself. "Is that what I did to Steve? Did I make him afraid?"

Noah reared back. "Good God, no. Maggie, no. Steve's death was nothing more than an accident."

"I know." She squeezed her eyes shut and twisted the towel tighter. "But did I make him think about fear, so that he wasn't concentrating on what he was doing? Did I, Noah?"

"You look at me, girl, and you look at me good."

The fierceness in his voice made her look.

"I wasn't talking about Steve," Noah said. "I was talking about Alex. They're not the same, Maggie, you know that. They might both be bull riders, but there's no two men more different than Steve and Alex. Nobody loved Steve more than I did, not even you. He was my boy, my baby. But hell, honey, you knew Steve. He was smart as a whip, but he still didn't have enough sense to be scared of anything. I was with him right before the ride. Believe me, fear was the farthest thing from his mind. He was out to have a good time, and that's all he was thinking about. What happened to him was an accident, and it had absolutely, positively nothing to do with you. Don't you ever think it did, you hear?"

She heard, but she was afraid to believe, afraid to let go of the guilt she'd carried so long.

"You hear?" Noah demanded.

In Noah's eyes she saw the truth. Something inside her shifted. That part of her that had held the guilt so close and tight relaxed, and before she could clench it to her in its old, familiar spot, the guilt slipped away, leaving her feeling odd and light.

Noah gave her a sharp nod. "That's better. Now. What did Alex have to say when you lit into him like you did?"

Maggie swallowed. "He just looked away real fast. And then he said he hoped he hadn't inherited his nerve from his father."

At Noah's sharp curse Maggie jerked her head up.

"*That's* what he meant," Noah said, his eyes wide. "Good God."

"What, Noah? What?"

"I thought it was funny, him signin' up for the rodeo when he looked like it was the last thing in the world he wanted to do. I was there, you know, when he signed up. Asked him afterward why he'd done it, what he was tryin' to prove." Noah shook his head.

Maggie felt cold all over. "What did he say?"

Noah's blue eyes pierced her. "Said he was trying to prove he could still do it."

It didn't make sense to Maggie. Nothing made sense. "Do what?"

"Ride bulls."

"I don't understand."

"Neither did I at the time. But him saying that about his father today . . ."

"Tell me, Noah. What about his father? What does that have to do with anything?"

Noah poured himself a cup of coffee and sat at the

table. "Lee Dillon was one of the best rodeo riders this county's ever seen. And horses, why you never saw a man better at training horses than Lee. That's where Alex gets it, I reckon. 'Course I've only seen Alex with one horse, but my guess is he's got the same knack his daddy did."

"What happened to Mr. Dillon?"

Noah shook his head again. "Nobody knows. He just up and disappeared one day, oh, years ago. Alex must have still been a kid then."

"I still don't understand. What does that have to do with Alex and bull riding?"

Noah looked her in the eye, and another chill raced down her spine. "Speculation was that Lee Dillon left town, left his wife and son to fend for themselves, because he'd lost his nerve."

The coldness spread from her spine to her stomach. "Lost his nerve?"

"Had a heck of a wreck one day over at the Heart of America Rodeo in Shawnee. Bull threw him and stomped him up pretty good. He never had the nerve to get back on another bull again. Way I recollect it, he never even rode a horse after that. Started drinkin' real bad, then a few weeks later, just up and disappeared."

There are things you don't understand . . . things I can't explain.

Where do you get your nerve?

Let's just hope I didn't inherit it from my old man.

Maggie covered her mouth with her hands and stared at Noah, horrified. "Oh, my God. Noah! He's *afraid!*"

Noah held her gaze. "And trying to prove he's not."

She dropped her hands to the table. "But *why?* If he's afraid, why doesn't he just *quit*, damn him? He doesn't have to prove anything to anybody."

"Yes, he does, Maggie girl. He has to prove it to himself. A man's gotta know, deep inside—he's gotta be able to look himself in the mirror every day and *know* he's not a coward."

"Alex is no coward!"

"I know that, and you know that. But Alex still has to prove it to himself."

"By climbing on the back of one of the meanest creatures God ever created? That's ridiculous."

"No it's not!" Noah cried. "Not to Alex. It's important to him. He's got to do it, Maggie, and you've got to let him. Don't you go tryin' to talk him out of it. Even if you could, he'd never be able to face himself again, because he wouldn't *know*. And a man's gotta know, Maggie girl. A man's gotta know."

Maggie lay in bed with her ears straining to hear the sound of Alex's pickup crunching gravel beneath its tires, but it was three in the morning and the sound hadn't come. Her fear lay next to her in the bed like a block of ice and made her shiver.

She couldn't let Alex go into that arena tomorrow without seeing him. She couldn't.

Yet what would she say to him? She would probably do something stupid, like beg him not to ride, even knowing that was the worst thing she could do to him now.

But damn it, she *loved* him. She would die a thousand deaths tomorrow waiting to learn if he'd been injured.

Then there was her secret fear that she hadn't really acknowledged since talking with Noah. What if Alex realized he *hadn't* lost his nerve? What if he got captured again by that thrill he'd told her about? What if he started riding again in every rodeo that came along? How would she stand it?

She wouldn't. She couldn't. Her fear was too great.

But then there was another fear. The fear of spending the rest of her life without Alex.

Her fear of the rodeo, of bull riding, was something she had known since Steve's first serious accident ten years ago when he'd broken his collarbone. It was a fear she had lived with every day since. It was a familiar fear, her constant companion. Sometimes, God help her, it was so familiar it was almost comfortable. How could she let go of something she had hugged close to her breast for so many years?

The same way you let go of your guilt today.

Okay, okay. Maybe. Maybe she could let go of her fear. But if she did, if she *could*, what would she have left to hold on to?

Alex. She might have Alex.

Yet with Alex, she would always fear anyway, so what would be different?

She could have her fear and be alone, or she could have her fear *and* Alex. If he would still have her after the way she had treated him this past week.

The question in her heart came down to which fear— the one with Alex, or without him, or for him—would be the most bearable.

But the question was moot. Her biggest fear was letting Alex walk into that arena tomorrow with her taunt about his nerve and broken bones ringing in his ears.

She crawled out of bed and went to the window, even knowing it was useless, and it was. He wasn't home. It looked like he wasn't coming home at all.

She paced the floor. Where was he? What was he

thinking? "Alex, I love you. No matter what happens, I love you."

But could she keep seeing him if he kept riding bulls? She honestly didn't believe she would be able to stand that kind of fear.

Saturday morning there was still no sign of Alex.

"What am I going to do, Noah? I can't let him ride without telling him I'm sorry. What am I going to do?"

Noah looked at her gravely. "You know what you're gonna do, Maggie girl. You just haven't admitted it yet."

The lump of fear in her stomach turned to ice. "You think I should go to the rodeo."

Noah gave a slight shrug. "That's up to you."

She shivered and hugged herself. "I haven't been to a rodeo since Steve's accident. I don't think I can do it, Noah."

"Maggie girl." Noah shook his head. "I guess you're just never gonna figure this one out on your own, so I'll have to butt in."

"What are you talking about?"

"I'm talking about your fear of the rodeo, bulls, horses, all of it."

She stiffened. "What is it you think I'm supposed to figure out?"

"Let me ask you a question," he said. "Suppose Steve hadn't been thrown from that bull. Suppose he'd walked away that afternoon, like he always had before, and had come on home to dinner. Suppose the next day he'd driven into town and got himself killed in a car accident right in the middle of Main Street."

"He didn't die in a car accident," Maggie cried. "It was the damned rodeo and you know it."

"Yeah, but if it *had* been a car accident, I'm just

wondering how the devil you'd be gettin' back and forth to town every day."

Maggie blinked. "What are you talking about?"

"I'm talking about your damn fear of the rodeo. If Steve had died in a car accident—people do, you know, dozens, probably hundreds of them every day—would you have said all cars are dangerous killers? Hellfire, a heck of a lot more people get killed in car wrecks than rodeos. What if one of them had been Steve? Would you forbid the kids to ever get around a car? Would you never go into town again because that's the place Steve got killed? Would you have sold your car and never set foot in another one all these years?"

"You're being ridiculous."

"That," he said poking a finger at her chest, "is precisely my point, girl."

THIRTEEN

Alex groaned and rolled over. For a startling second that brought him wide awake, he met nothing but air. Then hard, cold floor rushed up to meet him. He grunted and swore.

He supposed landing on the floor was no more than he deserved. He should have gone home last night and slept in his own bed. The cracked vinyl couch in the office of the feed store was not only too damn narrow, but about three feet too short as well. Not the recommended way to spend the night before a bull ride.

He should have gone home. Well, he did go home, actually. But "go" wasn't an accurate word for what he'd done. He'd snuck home the minute he'd left the café, because it was the only time he could be sure Maggie wouldn't be home. He'd grabbed clean clothes and his bag of gear for the bull ride and snuck right back out.

He'd been too chicken to risk running into Maggie.

Was this a sign that he really was turning into a first-class coward? Afraid to even face the woman he loved?

No. He wouldn't let himself believe that. Not yet. Besides, part of the reason he was making this ride today was for Maggie.

What an ass, Dillon. It wasn't for Maggie. It was for *him*. He could tell himself he couldn't ask to share Maggie's life until he was sure of himself, but the truth was, she might not want him anyway.

His stomach gave a sudden lurch at the thought.

But he couldn't afford to think about Maggie. Not today. Today he had to ride a bull. For the first time in his life, he didn't think he even cared if he won, just as long as he had the guts to ride.

He had to make only one ride. The Deep Fork Rodeo bull riding was a "one-go" event, no second or third round.

Just one ride. That's all he needed. Could he do it?

He would know the answer before the ride even started.

He stood up and changed into clean clothes, ignoring the chilly air in the office. Then he pulled his duffel bag between his feet and checked the contents again. Chaps, spurs, his right-hand glove, a leather thong, rosin, his bull rope.

He straightened up and stretched his back. Damn stupid thing to do, sleep on a too-short couch the night before a ride.

Coffee. Maybe coffee would get him going.

Alex arrived at the arena a good half-hour before the grand entry march. He wouldn't ride in that today. He had another ride on his mind. He leaned against the steel pipe fence around the arena and took in the familiar sights. Red, white, and blue bunting decorated the fencing, interspersed with advertising banners. Banners and bunting alike flapped and popped in the slight breeze.

The weather was perfect, with bright sun in a clear blue sky. Warmer than it should be, thank God, for the week before Thanksgiving.

Dust already flew thick in the air. It would only get worse as the day progressed.

Children ran beneath the wooden bleachers, shrieking and riding imaginary bucking broncs. Rodeo participants, men and women, mingled on horseback and on foot, greeting each other with friendly smiles and shouts. Members of the Deep Fork Roundup Club gathered on horseback to prepare for the grand entry.

Familiar sights, sounds, and smells. Alex had grown up with them, known them all his life. Nothing frightening here.

Not yet.

The bleachers were filling. He located the rodeo secretary and paid his fifty-dollar entry fee. The woman with the cash box at her elbow grinned at him. "Howdy. Hank said he'd talked you into ridin' today."

Hank. One of the men who'd come to the feed store and cornered him.

"I'm Martha Sedgewick, his mother. We're glad to have you."

Alex nodded. "Who'd I draw?"

Martha Sedgewick checked her list and let out a low whistle. "Don't look now, but you drew The Terminator. Been out of the chute at least twenty-five times and only been ridden twice. Real rank, from what I hear." She looked up at him through thick glasses. "Give him hell, Alex."

"Thanks, ma'am." He gave a tug on his hat brim, then headed for the pens.

The Terminator. Great. Just what he needed. The rankest bull around, who'd only been ridden twice.

Three of the five men who had come to his store to sign him up stood at the bull pens. Hank was among them, as was the tall one who'd taunted him about his last injury.

Hank let out a low whistle just like the one his mother had given. "I gotta tell ya, Dillon, I'm jealous as hell. I'd give anything to have a shot at The Terminator."

"You've seen him in action?" Alex asked.

"Have I ever. That son of a gun's got moves you won't believe. He'll jar your backbone so damn hard you'll be three inches shorter after the ride—if you make the ride."

"And he turns counterclockwise," the tall one warned. "Until you get your balance. Then he'll switch on you and turn his ass-end the other direction."

"Which one is he?" Alex asked.

"That one."

Alex stared at the one they indicated, one of the biggest Brahmas he'd ever seen, with sharp ten-inch horns sticking straight out of his head sideways. The slight forward curl at each deadly point would be just right to rip a man to shreds.

The reddish brown coat gleamed dully in the sun, especially where the light hit the hump between The Terminator's shoulders. The bull had more white on his face than most, with a red splotch beneath each eye. Maybe that was Mother Nature's attempt to make the eyes look bigger, kinder. The trick didn't work. Those damn eyes looked meaner than sin as the bull glared back at Alex.

"Hear he weighs in at two thousand twelve pounds," someone said.

Hank let out another whistle.

As the others told him everything they knew about The Terminator, Alex waited for the fear to come. It didn't. But then, he wasn't in the chute with that brute yet either.

With his fear on hold, so to speak, Alex relaxed into the conversation and shared what he knew of the bulls the others had drawn while Hank pinned Alex's entry number to the back of his shirt.

The parade passed through the arena, followed by the national anthem, then the rodeo officially started. The bull riding would, as always, be last, but Alex and the others started getting ready. And still, he waited. Waited for the locking of muscles, the breath stopping in his chest, his gut tightening with fear.

But not yet. Not yet.

He breathed easier and pulled his chaps from his duffel bag. He strapped them on, then his spurs. He grabbed his bull rope, rosin, glove, and the thong to tie the glove to his wrist. After several minutes of ritual stretching to warm up his leg muscles, he left the bag on the ground beside the pen and worked his way toward the bull chutes. He mentally ran over everything the others had told him about The Terminator, trying to imagine every move the bull would make and how to ride through each attempt to dislodge him.

Alex was the last rider on the list, one man he didn't know just before him, with Hank third from last.

Alex had ridden Big Mac, the bull Hank had drawn. Mac wasn't as ornery as some, but ornery enough to give a cowboy a good ride. "Watch that right twist of his," Alex warned, "just before he snaps left."

Hank worked the bull rope around his gloved hand and nodded. "Will do." When he was satisfied his grip on the bull rope was tight enough, he made ready to lower himself onto Big Mac's back. "Okay!"

Hank dropped to the bull's back. The cowbell hanging from the bottom of the bull rope clanked. The gate of the chute flew open, and the bull thundered out bucking and snorting and leaping and doing everything in his power to throw off the unwelcome weight on his back.

The crowd roared. The two clowns, one a barrel man, the other a bullfighter, stuck close to the bull, leaped with him, danced with him, lunged with him, ready at a second's notice to distract him with waves and shouts and antics should the rider be thrown. A bull rider's best friends, those clowns. They'd saved more than a few necks.

Alex glanced at the clock. Four seconds. Five seconds. Six. Damn, but eight seconds was a hell of a long time. An eternity for someone in Hank's position. Seven.

Then suddenly the bull did exactly what Alex had warned Hank about. He threw his head to the right and gave a sharp jerk, then snapped left. Hank, holding the rope in his right hand, flew off on the bull's left side, "in the well." The worst place a rider could be, except for beneath the hooves, because from that angle, he couldn't work his hand free of the bull rope.

Alex gripped the top rail. "Come on, Hank, hold on, they're coming."

Hank flopped helplessly against Big Mac's head and shoulder. The clowns moved in, one waving and shouting, the other coming from the right to try to free Hank's hand while the bull kept on bucking and leaping.

The crowd jumped to its feet as if following a choreographer's lead. Their combined gasps echoed across the arena, then silence. The only sounds were those of the bull, the cowbell clanking between and just behind his front legs, the clowns, and Hank, grunting every time he landed against the bull.

Dust, churned to a thick cloud by the bull's hooves and by the clowns, nearly obscured the action completely.

Finally the clown was able to reach in and jerk the rosined bull rope loose, and Hank dropped to the ground like a limp rag. The bull pawed the ground and lowered his head, turning from side to side, trying to decide whether to go for the man on the ground or the one waving and shouting at him.

When it looked like the bull was about to make for the clown, the gate to the bull pen at the far end of the arena flew open and the bull headed straight for it like a trained puppy.

Alex relaxed his grip on the rail. In less than a minute Big Mac was out of the arena, Hank was climbing to his feet, and the next rider was getting ready.

The announcer's voice came, tinny sounding, from the loudspeakers. *"He's all right, folks. Number seventeen Hank Sedgewick is all right. No score for the young man, but let's put our hands together and give the local cowboy a big round of applause. Next up . . ."*

Then it would be Alex's turn.

He felt his heart pounding. Fear? Maybe, but not for himself. Not yet. This was for Hank, for the poor guy ending up "in the well," as he had. A damn bad place to be, Alex knew.

With bull rope in hand, Alex made his way to chute number three. The Terminator was there waiting for him. With blood in his eye. "We're next, ol' boy," Alex told him. "Just you and me."

Alex slipped on his right glove, then pulled the

leather thong from his pocket and wrapped it tight around his wrist to keep the glove from slipping off during the ride. Then he climbed up over the side of the chute and braced his feet on each side of the gate, keeping his weight off the bull for now. He wasn't about to put his legs between two thousand plus pounds of Brahma and the solid walls of the chute.

Two men helped him pull the bull rope and wrap it as tight as possible around the bull and Alex's right hand. The cowbell hanging beneath the bull clanked. The Terminator bellowed and reared up beneath Alex, nearly knocking him out of the chute.

Alex grabbed for the railing and laughed. "Don't like that bell much, huh, ol' fella? That's all right— you're not supposed to like it, you devil."

Alex gave another tug on the rope. Both rope and glove were heavily rosined. The strength of Alex's grip was the only thing that would keep him from flying off the bull's back the second the chute opened. The only help he had was the rosin. If the rope slipped from his hand, it would fall to the ground and Alex would fly through the air.

He did *not* want to fly through the air. A man had his dignity after all. Those were friends and neighbors out there in the stands. Many of them were his customers at the feed store. He was certain he would have a much more comfortable future if he didn't give them anything to snicker over.

No, he did not want to fly through the air. At least not until after the eight-second horn. After that, well, everybody knew the hardest, most dangerous part of the event wasn't riding the bull, it was getting off the damn mean son of a gun.

Alex gave another tug on the bull rope. Good. Tight.

"Whenever you're ready, Dillon," the man at the gate called.

Alex felt a slow grin coming on. It was only then that he remembered why he was about to drop his weight onto the back of one solid ton of something mean and alive and called The Terminator. He was supposed to be afraid. Or at least, he had thought he might be.

He threw his head back and laughed at his own useless worries. Damn, but he felt good. He'd forgotten to be afraid. He *wasn't* afraid. Not one damn bit.

Sure, his pulse pounded and his breath came fast in his chest. But that wasn't fear, it was sheer adrenaline. The best score so far was a seventy-eight for the tall rider whose name Alex still couldn't remember.

Damnation. He could beat that.

He laughed again at his own stupidity. He had put himself through hell for weeks. And Maggie. He stopped laughing. What had his foolishness done to Maggie?

He tugged his hat on tight and let his gaze scan the crowd. It was time to get this ride over with so he could go home to Maggie. Would she still want him? Would she take him back?

He stopped dead in the middle of lowering his hand. "Good God."

Maggie!

She sat near the top in the east bleachers. Her eyes looked wide with fear, her smile forced and frozen. *Maggie.*

What the *hell* was she doing here?

And Noah. *And the kids!* All three of them jumping up and down on the bleachers, waving and shouting at him. Even little Cindy.

The kids' being here was one thing. They'd probably

never been to a rodeo and thought it was fun. But Maggie? What the hell was she doing here? Had Noah made her come?

Ah, damn it, Maggie, why are you doing this to yourself?

Well, he wouldn't prolong her misery one second longer than necessary.

Dear God, don't let me get hurt while she's watching. Don't give her that to add to her nightmares.

Alex gave his hat another jerk, then centered his gaze on the Brahma's hump and raised his left hand in the air. At the same instant he let his weight down onto the bull's back, Alex nodded for the bull and shouted, "Let's go!"

Maggie bit her lower lip and clutched Noah's hand until her fingers ached. She had wanted to talk to Alex before his ride. But by the time she had made up her mind to come, then made up her mind to bring the kids, then had a flat tire on the van on the way to the arena, she had been too late. The events were half over, and the bull riding was coming up. She hadn't wanted to distract Alex with her own worries just before his ride.

Noah had been right. Coming to the rodeo wasn't the traumatic experience she had expected it to be. Yes, this very arena was where Steve died, and she would never forget that day as long as she lived. But she honestly didn't feel as though she was about to be treated to a repeat performance.

She had been to so many rodeos in her life that coming back after all these years was really more like visiting an old friend than reliving a nightmare. The ease she felt surprised her. And if she was honest with herself, it even disappointed her. Now she could not truthfully turn to Noah in fear and say, "I told you so. I told you I was too afraid to come here."

No, Noah already knew better. He'd been grinning at her since they arrived.

And the kids. They were loving every exciting minute of it. Stephen had come as a young child, but not since Steve's death. Now her oldest was lording it over the other two, explaining things, answering their questions. The little devil was passing himself off as a rodeo expert. He'd been five the last time he'd come.

Everything wasn't smooth and easy, however. Maggie had nearly swallowed her tongue when Hank Sedgewick had gone "in the well" instead of jumping off free of the bull. If he didn't have a separated shoulder, she'd eat her boots.

Then another man rode, and before she realized it, Alex was climbing into the chute at the north end of the arena. She held her breath. Would he be afraid? She didn't want him to be afraid. But she wasn't sure she wanted him to enjoy himself too much either. Enjoy himself so much he would start signing up for every rodeo that came along.

But she knew that was exactly what was happening when she saw him throw his head back and laugh. She couldn't see his eyes from this distance, but she knew they had to look a little wild, filled with excitement that vibrated right down to his toes.

Sounding like it was coming from a tin can, the announcer's voice blared over the loudspeakers. *"Our next rider up is another homegrown Lincoln County boy from Meeker, number twenty-three, Alex Dillon. Alex has had a fine career riding bulls. . . ."*

Maggie let the announcer's words fade and kept her gaze trained on Alex. Then he looked up and saw her.

"Look, Mom, it's Alex," Doug cried.

All three children jumped and waved and hollered. Maggie forced herself to smile and wondered what he was thinking just then to make his laughter die.

With a sharp motion, he gave a nod, tugged at his hat brim, and let out a shout. The chute flew open and Maggie's heart jumped up and lodged itself in her throat.

Two thousand pounds of angry bull came charging into the arena, bucking, leaping into the air, and coming down on stiff front legs, jarring Alex back and forth.

"*Look at Alex spur that bull, ladies and gentlemen. A bull rider's not required to spur, he's only required to hang on with one hand. But Alex is a wild one, he is . . .*"

Even though she held her breath, Maggie had to admire Alex's form and skill. He rode that bull as if he'd been doing it all his life, which he had, she knew. He kept his left arm high in the air and used it to keep his balance when the bull twisted and spun, trying to throw Alex off.

Three seconds. Four.

Maggie leaned forward. *Come on, Alex.*

Five.

She bit her lip harder and tasted blood.

Six.

Hang on, Alex, hang on!

Seven.

Maggie rose to her feet. "Ride him, Alex!"

Eight!

The horn sounded the end of the ride.

Maggie held her breath, knowing the most dangerous part was getting off the bull. The Terminator didn't have a "park" gear. He wasn't going to stop spinning and bucking so Alex could climb down.

But Maggie shouldn't have worried. Alex was a pro. Still in control, of himself if not the bull, he waited for the right instant, then let go of his bull rope and threw himself backward. His hat flew off. He landed on his shoulder behind the bull. The clowns waved and shouted to keep the bull from turning around while Alex got to his feet.

Maggie let out a breath, only then realizing how her knees trembled. She told herself to relax.

Too soon.

The bull charged one of the clowns. The clown wasn't quick enough, and the bull hit him square in the chest, lifting the clown clear off the ground with the flat of his head.

The second clown rushed the bull to distract him but tripped over the cowbell attached to Alex's bull rope lying in the dirt.

Someone in the stands screamed.

Maggie held her breath again as Alex—*Damn you, Alex, get out of there and let somebody else help!*— yelled and waved his arms to get the bull's attention away from the clowns.

The bull turned toward Alex and lowered his head. Sharp, deadly hooves pawed the ground and churned up more dust.

Maggie's ears rang with the sudden silence of the crowd. She put both hands over her mouth to keep from screaming.

Then the second clown, the one who had tripped, got up and taunted the bull.

The animal swung his lowered head from side to side, trying to pick his target.

Alex reached down and grabbed his hat from the dirt.

The bull charged.

Behind her hands, Maggie screamed.

Alex scrambled for the fence and made it to the top rail with less than half a second to spare before the bull rammed it head on and full speed. Alex jumped down on the outside of the fence. Maggie caught a glimpse of his face. She squeezed her eyes shut. She had never seen a man look so . . . alive, so excited.

She knew it now. He would surely be bull riding more often in the future.

Could she live with that? Just because she had watched him once didn't mean she had enjoyed it or it had been easy, didn't mean she would have the nerve to do it again.

"Did you see, Mom? Did you see that bull chase Alex?"

She put her hand on Doug's shoulder and hoped he wouldn't notice her trembling. "I saw, honey."

"Ladies and gentlemen, the judges have given Alex Dillon an eighty-five. That outstanding score makes him the winner of today's bull riding event. Let's put our hands together and give a big round of applause. . . ."

"He won! He won! Wasn't he great?" Stephen cried.

"Yeah." Maggie wanted to give her kids a cheerful smile, but somehow it just wouldn't come. "He was great."

With a deep breath, she turned to Noah. "I'll meet you and the kids at the van."

Noah squinted at her. "Where are you going?"

"I'm going to find Alex."

A slow grin came across Noah's weathered face. He nodded. "That's my girl."

As Maggie made her way down the bleachers and into the milling crowd, she had no idea what she was going to say to Alex. She only knew she had to make sure he was all right. It hadn't been that long since his left arm was in a sling—bruised shoulder muscles, she thought she remembered. And he had just landed on that same shoulder, hard.

On her way toward the back of the pens where she thought he would be, Maggie greeted the stunned looks of her friends and neighbors. Everyone knew how she felt about the rodeo since Steve's death. This was the last place anyone would expect to see her.

But that was in the past. She had proved to herself today that she could watch a rodeo without being terrified. Could watch the man she loved ride a bull.

The question now was, was she strong enough to do it again and again?

Then she saw Alex, surrounded by a group of cowboys congratulating him on his win, and she knew. She knew she loved him so much she could do whatever she had to in order to be near him.

Someone in front of Alex shifted sideways, and he saw her. He dropped his duffel bag and shouldered his way through the men, telling them something she couldn't hear.

He rushed toward her with anxious eyes. She saw his lips move. "Maggie."

When he reached her, he grasped her shoulders. "Are you all right?" he demanded fiercely. "What are you doing here? If Noah made you come, I'll—"

"No, no," she said. She placed her hands on his chest and felt his solid strength. "I came to see you ride. It's all right, Alex, really."

He studied her face closely. He must have found the answer he sought, for he closed his eyes and hugged her to him. "You'll never know how scared I was when I saw you in the stands. Maggie, Maggie, why did you put yourself through that?"

Maggie pushed away until she could see his face, cup it between her hands. "I wanted to see you before you rode, but I didn't get the chance. I wanted to tell you I was sorry for the way I've been acting, for the things I said yesterday."

"You could have told me later. You didn't have to put yourself through this."

"Yes," she said firmly, "I did. You had something you had to prove today, and so did I. And I think we both found our answers."

Alex frowned.

She caressed his jaw. "Noah told me about your father. You're not like him, Alex. I could have told you that."

He hugged her close again. "I had to know, Maggie. I had to find out."

"And what did you find out?"

He pulled his head back and looked at her. "I found out Cindy was right that day in the restaurant. I'm an idiot. I'm not my father. I don't need the bulls to make me feel like I'm worth the space I take up. I need you, Maggie. Just you."

With a glad cry, Maggie threw her arms around his neck. "I need you, too. And if you want to sign up for every damn rodeo that comes along, I'll be right there beside you, cheering you on every time."

"No," he said holding her close. "I don't want to ride bulls anymore. I don't need it, Maggie. Not anymore. I don't want it. I want . . ."

"You want?"

"I want to run the feed store. I want to raise and train my own horses. I want . . . Damn. This is a hell of a place to say something like this, but if I don't say it right now, I'll burst. I love you, Maggie. I love you."

She buried her face against his neck and fought tears. "I love you, too, so much. So much."

He pushed her far enough away that he could look her in the eye. "Do you love me enough to marry me?"

Maggie's heart gave a leap. "Is this a proposal?"

"You mean you can't tell?"

Maggie grinned.

Alex grinned, too. He dropped his arms from around her and stood back. "Margaret Suzanne Hazelwood Randolph, will you marry me?"

A catcall.

A wolf whistle.

Maggie ignored them and gazed into Alex's brown-black eyes. "Oh, Alex, *really*?"

Alex grinned. "Yes, Maggie. *Really*."

"What do you say, Maggie?" someone yelled.

"Hey, folks, we got us a marriage proposal goin' on over here."

More catcalls.

More whistles.

Maggie ignored the gathering crowd. With her heart pounding and her eyes stinging, she threw herself against Alex's chest. "Yes! Oh, yes. Alex, I love you."

"All right!" someone shouted.

And from the edge of the crowd, Maggie heard Noah's laughing voice. "Looky there, kids. You just got yourself a new daddy."

SHARE THE FUN...
SHARE YOUR NEW-FOUND TREASURE!!

You don't want to let your new books out of your sight? That's okay. Your friends can get their own. Order below.

No. 29 FOSTER LOVE by Janis Reams Hudson
Morgan comes home to claim his children but Sarah claims his heart.

No. 72 COMING HOME by Janis Reams Hudson
Clint always loved Lacey. Now Fate has given them another chance.

No. 103 FOR THE THRILL by Janis Reams Hudson
Maggie hates cowboys, *all* cowboys! Alex has his work cut out for him.

No. 56 A QUESTION OF VIRTUE by Carolyn Davidson
Neither Sara nor Cal can ignore their almost magical attraction.

No. 57 BACK IN HIS ARMS by Becky Barker
Fate takes over when Tara shows up on Rand's doorstep again.

No. 58 SWEET SEDUCTION by Allie Jordan
Libby wages war on Will—she'll win his love yet!

No. 59 13 DAYS OF LUCK by Lacey Dancer
Author Pippa Weldon finds her real-life hero in Joshua Luck.

No. 60 SARA'S ANGEL by Sharon Sala
Sara *must* get to Hawk. He's the only one who can help.

No. 61 HOME FIELD ADVANTAGE by Janice Bartlett
Marian shows John there is more to life than just professional sports.

No. 62 FOR SERVICES RENDERED by Ann Patrick
Nick's life is in perfect order until he meets Claire!

No. 63 WHERE THERE'S A WILL by Leanne Banks
Chelsea goes toe-to-toe with her new, unhappy business partner.

No. 64 YESTERDAY'S FANTASY by Pamela Macaluso
Melissa always had a crush on Morgan. Maybe dreams do come true!

No. 65 TO CATCH A LORELEI by Phyllis Houseman
Lorelei sets a trap for Daniel but gets caught in it herself.

No. 66 BACK OF BEYOND by Shirley Faye
Dani and Jesse are forced to face their true feelings for each other.

No. 67 CRYSTAL CLEAR by Cay David
Max could be the end of all Crystal's dreams . . . or just the beginning!

No. 68 PROMISE OF PARADISE by Karen Lawton Barrett
Gabriel is surprised to find that Eden's beauty is not just skin deep.

No. 69 OCEAN OF DREAMS by Patricia Hagan
Is Jenny just another shipboard romance to Officer Kirk Moen?

No. 70 SUNDAY KIND OF LOVE by Lois Faye Dyer
Trace literally sweeps beautiful, ebony-haired Lily off her feet.

No. 71 ISLAND SECRETS by Darcy Rice
Chad has the power to take away Tucker's hard-earned independence.

No. 73 KING'S RANSOM by Sharon Sala
Jesse was always like King's little sister. When did it all change?

No. 74 A MAN WORTH LOVING by Karen Rose Smith
Nate's middle name is 'freedom' . . . that is, until Shara comes along.

No. 75 RAINBOWS & LOVE SONGS by Catherine Sellers
Dan has more than one problem. One of them is named Kacy!

No. 76 ALWAYS ANNIE by Patty Copeland
Annie is down-to-earth and real . . . and Ted's never met anyone like her.

No. 77 FLIGHT OF THE SWAN by Lacey Dancer
Rich had decided to swear off romance for good until Christiana.

Meteor Publishing Corporation
Dept. 892, P. O. Box 41820, Philadelphia, PA 19101-9828

Please send the books I've indicated below. Check or money order (U.S. Dollars only)—no cash, stamps or C.O.D.s (PA residents, add 6% sales tax). I am enclosing $2.95 plus 75¢ handling fee for *each* book ordered.

Total Amount Enclosed: $_____.

___ No. 29	___ No. 59	___ No. 65	___ No. 71
___ No. 72	___ No. 60	___ No. 66	___ No. 73
___ No. 103	___ No. 61	___ No. 67	___ No. 74
___ No. 56	___ No. 62	___ No. 68	___ No. 75
___ No. 57	___ No. 63	___ No. 69	___ No. 76
___ No. 58	___ No. 64	___ No. 70	___ No. 77

Please Print:
Name _____
Address _____ Apt. No. _____
City/State _____ Zip _____

Allow four to six weeks for delivery. Quantities limited.